MW00682083

THE

TREE

TATTOO

THE TREE TATTOO

KAREN RIVERS

The publisher gratefully acknowledges the support of the Canada Council for the Arts and the Ontario Arts Council for its publishing program. We acknowledge the financial support of the Government of Canada through the Book Publishing Industry Development Program (BPIDP) for our publishing activities.

Canada

Printed and bound in Canada.

Canadian Cataloguing in Publication Data

Rivers, Karen, 1970-
The tree tattoo

ISBN 1-896951-16-3

I. Title.

PS8585.I8778T74 1999 C831'.54 C99-900988-5
PR9199.3.R48T74 1999

Cormorant Books Inc.
RR 1, Dunvegan, Ontario K0C 1J0

For everyone who believed in me,
encouraged me, and supported me —
especially my parents, my sisters,
and, of course, Tim.

PROLOGUE

In the silence of life, a sudden noise.

Words are spoken softly and with melody, comforting. Melanoma, carcinoma, malignancy, monogamy, and lymphoma contain the syllables of a spreading cancer, a lilting poetry that says only death. Words too harsh for English, disguised by Latin and Greek, languages that are insects: *Nymphalis antiopa*, a butterfly called "mourning cloak".

This is a curse, drifting from the bitter thoughts of the wronged wife to the girl who has stolen what the wife never had. The girl. How innocent a word — better "tramp". Or harlot. Slut. Bitch. Nothing is harsh enough. No words can paint an accurately painful picture, complete with bleeding, raw flesh torn from the bone.

The doctor's words are imprecise, they do not tell the whole story, the inevitable ending is what the girl sees in his expression, the way his hand twists his wristwatch back and forth, throwing a small prismatic circle of light onto the wall beside the steel sink. The girl focuses on the tiny rainbow bobbing around on the whiteness. His nebulous murmurs speak only of the need for haste, a consultation, operations and options. Optional operations.

His words are heavy and roll towards her like heavy boulders on a grassy slope, green grass that is so rich and scented it should be food, dripping with nutrients. The grass muffles what the doctor is trying to say, but still he talks. The rainbow darts around the white wall. The girl is thinking, wait, this cannot happen to me. This is a disease of the old and disenchanted; the unhealthy middle-aged, with skin loose like nylons washed too many times hanging hopelessly around swollen ankles. This is not a disease for young people. Young girls. Me.

This morning, there was nothing. Or something, maybe, but little more than a thought. A slight bulge around her middle, the absence of her period, the swelling of her breasts. She was almost sure — a baby, sweet pink and innocent like a bud on a plum tree in spring. She was pleased. This bulge, this baby, was hers and hers alone. This swelling somehow might wipe the slate clean.

Irony steals into her veins with cold creeping certainty. Her life, and death, is about to become ironic in a way that seems too cruel to be real. Her thoughts swing to the wife. Bitch, she thinks, you did this.

The girl was made to wait for a long time before seeing the doctor, this man who is insisting on spelling out her doom in his language which she has long ago stopped attempting to interpret. The girl is thinking now, I should have left. While perched on the acid-green vinyl chair in the waiting room, her gaze had repeatedly drifted to the window, where the sky was clear and awash with a cold breeze. She pressed her hand against the hard knot in her belly and smiled benevolently around the room, her pink cheeks a symbol of her youthful good health. Through her jeans, she traced her fingers up and down the corded muscle of her thighs, feeling her strength, her beauty. My body is a machine, she thought, my body is a temple. My body will house this baby, feed this baby. And then she was almost overcome by panic: joy and grief entangled deeply in her heart.

A baby will ruin everything.

She waited. Time slid by with elaborate languor. The room was warm, tinged with antiseptic and the freshly watered soil at the base of withered plants. Occasionally, she noticed the doctor slide by silent as an eel, passing back and forth from one room to another, one file to the next. For periods of time, he remained an echo of a voice, behind closed doors. Her mind translated this echo into fully formed dialogues. She thought he was talking about golf, about fishing. A glistening of irritation began to grow.

She could have left, so easily, stepped out into the cleansing slap of spring air. She could have driven away. She could have not known.

She imagines herself climbing into her car, warmed inside by the early pale sun, and driving away. She yearns for the feel of the road squirting from beneath the smooth rotation of the tires. Now it is too late, of course, the words have been spoken, the lump has been palpated, analysed. Hours have passed without notice, she has moved mechanically, politely, between floors. To the lab. To X-ray. To the office of a colleague for another opinion. Another worried gaze.

Blood has been drawn. A fate has been decided.

She could have driven away — believing for nine months at least — a baby. Carefully drinking whole milk and orange juice, choosing names from paperback books. She yearns to go back in time, change the outcome.

Now she is expected to go home, go to a hospital, expose her body to the surgeon's steel. She has a handful of papers. Thank you, she says to the doctor, a half-smile playing at her lips. He touches her arm, too gently, his touch like a nail dragged down a chalkboard. A symphony of brass instruments playing in a minor key is crashing through her veins. The sound is so loud in her ears that she touches them tentatively, half expecting to feel blood. Her high heels make a distinct, yet uneven, clip clop on the linoleum floor in the hallway that is suddenly miles long. She steps heavily on her half-healed ankle to feel the pain she understands snapping up her leg like a small dog's bite. An endless walk — she wants to drop to her knees and feel the cold waxiness against her cheek and smell cleaning fluid and other people's leather. She wants to scream and cry and have someone hold her and say, it will be all right. You'll be all right.

But of course, there is no one left.

Instead, the half-smile is affixed almost dreamily to her lips, and she holds the door open for the elderly gentleman slouched so far over his cane his nose seems only inches from his knees. She walks out of the office into the resounding air, everything in front of her appearing in colours too bright, false fluorescent sun. Her skull hums with something that must be terror.

The hospital, one o'clock. The beginning of the cloak of disease filters reality further and further away.

Soon the singing will begin, chorus and verse, discordant and harsh, in the key of C, standing on a cliff in winter, on the clearest day of the year.

Carcinoma. Malignancy. Rigor mortis. Post mortem.

The girl slips behind the wheel of the car. She speaks out loud to the emptiness:

This song is for you, the wife. You who will probably remain pink-cheeked and healthy to a forbidding age. Smoking, drinking, never exercising, it won't matter. You have been blessed, given health, pure clean good health, health that courses through your veins as cold and sparkling as water dripping from the edge of a glacier. You don't know me. You never did.

The girl curses the wife.

I give you this story, she says, her voice like tiny pieces of coral, breaking underfoot. I will give you this story.

Scribo ut supersum. I write that I may survive.

Chapter 1

Winter begins early. Blame this on El Niño. It is not even December, and it is freezing. The colour has been sucked from the sky and the city is a blank canvas, awaiting a painter to give it colour. That is the kind of day it is: a pale wash of grey, the thick wool of fog blurring all the harsh edges like Vaseline smeared on a camera lens.

The sharks are coming farther and farther north. Some have been seen as far north as Washington state, where the water is now ridiculously warm. Blame this on El Niño as well.

Today is the day that the girl and the man break open the warm, comfortable egg of friendship and find inside the rich yellow yolk of lust and possibility. Today is that day. Imagine.

It is a day spent, mostly, waiting.

Outside, breathe the white cold sky that stings skin and leaves words hanging in the air. Freshened by new ice, it is sharp and fresh and jagged. Each lungful tastes clear and precise, a bell ringing at the back of the throat. Be careful: December's grey spirit marches through the busy streets creating stealthy patches of black ice and unscrapable frost on windshields and windows. The wind blows as though cold is the only temperature it knows, as though there were no spring coming.

There is no spring coming.

Look at the trees:

Naked, they stand, fragile and beautiful, in anticipation of any sudden wrath of wind and snow. They stretch their iron-lace branches up towards the darkened sky, towards the frigid finality of the endless season. Survivors, they stand in wait. Wait for spring. Wait for rain.

Wait.

The man admires the stark beauty of the trees both stripped and evergreen that ebb and flow in undulating rows and patches over his acres of land. His land. His trees. Feel the trunk of a white birch, impossibly smooth and cold. The man allows the sap from a still-vibrant Douglas fir to stick to his fingers, breathes deeply the scent of pine and spruce. The quiet is palpable.

Breathe.

His land echoes in his lungs, thick with the scent of soil and bark and peace and solitude. He walks a while, pausing to look at the Christmas trees blowing and rustling in the breeze. This year he has made a mistake, relenting to the pressure of his more business-minded sons, allowing them to convince him to sell Christmas trees. Christmas trees. He shakes his head at the cruelty of the whole thing, the disposability that people love so much. Enjoy a thing, then throw it out. Recycle, that will make it all right, the waste. People will soon come and go, one small ready-to-die tree their reward for the long drive from town. He cringes. Shakes his head, feels his thoughts shift and move like a pile of leaves in fall, stirred by biting autumn winds.

From where he stands, the sounds of the city are beyond muted, they simply don't exist at all. His eyes roam, then settle on his house, a mile down the hill. Squint — it makes it easier to see. The brown building swims unwillingly into focus. If he could only squint hard enough, he could see through the windows, through the walls. He could see his wife, watching talk shows, reading, knitting. At one time, she used to paint, paint for hours, whirling and twirling the paint across canvas. Bright thick orgasmic colours. Her hand would dance, so intricate and beautiful, weaving stories on the easel. The trees in all their gnarled beauty appeared like magic from the tip of her thoughts onto the clean white canvas. His wife, tongue peeking out between lips in concentration, painting like a dream.

Then, nothing.

Oh, first she stopped trees but tried houses, buildings, churches, people, kids, pets. The abrupt stop was so sudden it was almost a sound, like a thunderclap, or a door slamming.

The children moved away, as children do, as you teach them to do, and his wife folded in on herself, an old woman. The paints dried to a crust in the cupboard, curled up in tiny tubes. Cerulean blue. Meadow gold. Carmine red. Snow white.

When did he become old enough to have a wife that knits, each stitch marking off his age, her age, every sweater making him an old man? Old.

So quickly it happens!

The body slithers and slides unrestrained down the hill towards death. Slam on the brakes. Stop. His sigh hovers delicately in front of him, a hummingbird, and he lets the thought freeze and drop to the ground to shatter.

Halfway across town, the girl stares out the window into the silky grey haze of the day. It is her birthday. She is twenty-three years old.

She has told no one.

Who would she tell?

She cannot tell the man, who believes her to be older. Who obviously tells himself that she is older. Fool. How much older could she be? Clear tight skin, breasts that point up instead of down, no grey to contaminate her black curls. She still gets acne, a teenager's plight. How old does he think she is? Early twenties, late twenties. Thirty. What does it matter?

She would be older, for him, if she could. Reach into the jar of years and draw out something less unsettling. Thirty-five to his fifty-two? Forty? What would make it right?

His daughter, Jamie, is two years older than the girl. This makes her slightly queasy. This makes it seem unclean, perverse. However, it does not make it go away.

It, being, of course, the thing between them that she cannot name.

She imagines *it* to be a beast, a dragon spitting fire, encased in scales. She thinks of *it* as an eiderdown of the plushest feathers, wrapping around them tightly, irrefutably, trapping them. She knows *it* won't disappear: *it* is a cobweb, having both reached out and touched *it* they are now hopelessly entwined, stuck until something breaks the threads.

The nameless thing: *it*.

The power of it.

We have to talk about it.

We should think about it.

We will be consumed by it.

All, of course, not said. Things left unsaid are the most dangerous, the most exciting. Sharks swim silently closer under the cover of water, listening for vibrations, tasting fear. The man is coming over. Tonight, what is between them will become fully formed, they will give it substance.

Feed the flames of the beast. Her imagination roars. Her foot taps the floor in anticipation, impatience.

Capture the details:

The fine web of lines around his eyes that ripple inwards when he smiles, the way his hair has faded in patches to silver that shines metallic in the light of the sun, the square-cut fingernails nestled in fingers strangely long and artistic with a pianist's grace, the timbre of his voice when he speaks, the tremor in his voice when he speaks to the girl. He gets nervous — words tripping over each other — when he notices how closely she is paying attention. When he notices how she looks at his mouth when he talks, at his hands, at his eyes.

She makes him nervous. Does this give her power?

Since the first time she saw him, she has wanted to curl up in his arms and lose herself in the folds of his skin. She has wanted to sink into his warmth and his smell, so rich and thick and solid. Sometimes, she forgets to hear what he is saying, she is too enraptured by his being.

The girl thinks this is love. *It.*

Today is her birthday, a day to celebrate. Twenty-three. Entering her twenty-fourth year, this same heart, these same lungs, this same mind. Time is snapping up her youth, she can feel the corrosion of age beginning to change the texture of her skin, the squeaking of her joints. At twenty-three, she feels ageless, ancient, afraid, impossibly young. Twenty-three going on seventy-five. Twenty-three going on fourteen.

Abandoning all pretence of working, she layers on mismatched sweats and socks, gloves and hat. Run. Down the stairs, careful not to slip on unsalted wood. She steps down and takes off as though a starting gun has propelled her off the blocks, her razor-sharp body slices through the swathe of winter, a jagged tear on the horizon.

Look up:

A few heavy clouds traipse across the winter sky with dogged determination, spreading chill as far as the eye can see.

Breathe.

The air snaps in and out of her lungs, stinging at first, then searing. She imagines needles of ice puncturing through lung into bloodstream, her eyes stream with tears not from pain but from the silver blades of the wind. All the while her feet grind down the salt on the sidewalks, slipping away when invisible ice wrenches her knees and back as she fights to stay upright.

Stumbling.

Slipping.

She is clumsy. Momentarily, she wants to stop, to lie down, to allow the whiteness of the day to swirl around her in a dizzy fog, feel the cold leap through her sweat-soaked back.

Stop?

Never. She comes to the park and runs along the grass, legs stretched to their full extension, feels the galloping power a horse must feel, savours the gentle crunch of the frosted grass, breathes in the smell of the vast empty nothingness and becomes reborn.

Finds her rhythm in this endless sparkling field, slides into the dance of the run and loses herself in its hypnotic syncopation. Floats free of herself. Her feet thud against the frozen earth for hours, every joint in her body crying out in ecstasy peppered so strongly with pain that she is a violin being played with the strings too tight, still running until she knows one of those strings will snap and break if she does not stop.

Run away.

Run forward. Or back.

Run.

It is what defines the girl.

The man, too, is breathless. He has walked down to the house from the peak of the hill, where he carefully examined the maturing monk pines and blue spruce, monitored the accumulations of ice. The trees will survive. They were designed to survive. People are a different matter. Houses. Wives.

He opens the front door, which has never been locked, and feels the solid punch of the oil heater, bringing beads of sweat to his forehead, making his lungs heavy. Up the stairs, to the left, he can see his wife leaning back in a kitchen chair, telephone receiver balancing between shoulder and chin, coffee in one hand, cigarette in the other. He notices — which is strange from such a distance with his poor eyesight — that the pores in her skin seem magnified, her makeup looks garish, clown-like, her body from the side doughy and misshapen. She laughs. Her voice is shrill and scrapes a part of him, too sharply. He gives himself absolution in this moment, with this snapshot. Permission.

This is not the woman he married: she was young and firmly fleshed and smelled clean and unmarred. Now, noticing as if for the first time the smoky, painted caricature that she has become, a smile creeps over his face. She smiles back, nodding, no break in her conversation.

Time slides by in handfuls.

In the bathroom that he built himself, the man looks at his reflection through the mirror's forgiving fog. When he thinks of the girl, he forgets he is a man, an old man, past middle age. He becomes, again, a schoolboy, falling in love for the first time. The first kiss. First touch. There is a tight thread being pulled through his heart, causing each beat to sing, a note held strong and full inside his chest. Her skin will be so soft and warm, her hair so thick and heavy. His body lurches deep inside. He stares at his own face, rubs a spot clear in the glass so he can see better.

Wait.

No.

Old eyes stare back, unblinking — lizard eyes trapped in folds of reptilian skin. The air that all morning has cushioned his steps falls flat and he becomes ridiculous, staring into that mirror, seeing his own greying face staring back. What could she possibly want with a ghost of a man like him?

There must be some mistake.

Shake your head clear. Cold water splashed on skin can be startling. Shock yourself back into youth. Don't think too carefully about it.

He allows the waiting and the shower and the lying and the dinner which he cannot taste to propel him safely towards evening and the girl.

Safely.

Showered and clean, the girl cannot decide what to wear. Lingerie, too obvious. Sweats, too casual. A dress, too formal. She will still be wearing her robe when he arrives, but she does not know that now. She picks up one outfit after another, dismissing, refolding, re-hanging. She goes through every stitch in her closet, feels giddy and unsure and terrified and silly. Forces herself to come back down from her skittish high, allows herself a drink of soothing amber Scotch, feels it flowing down her throat like oil, loosening muscles, heating. An adult drink.

Relax.

Standing at the window she listens as her heart pours blood through her body, then draws it back in. Listens to oxygen exploding into her cells, carbon dioxide flowing from her lungs. To her, the sound of the body is better than any music, silence in which she can hear herself living is the most beautiful orchestra of all.

Now, she thinks, is the winter of our discontent. She has long since forgotten which Shakespearean play spawned the quote, nonetheless, staring out the leaded glass window, she thinks of it. Now is the winter of our discontent. Now. It is like a song she can't break free from, repeating over and over again, a record with the needle stuck deep into one groove.

She steps back into the white room, falling into shadows as the promise of evening glimmers. Twilight is flirting with the headlights of traffic streaming by, creating splotches of pooled light on the wall behind her, circles floating and hovering in mid-air. Every once in a while a shadow car, unlit, will slip by on the wet roads reflected in someone else's beams, breaking the solid chain. A chain is only as strong as its weakest link, she thinks.

I am a weak link.

Now is the winter of our discontent.

So many people, blurring by in their own private haste. What does it matter what she is doing? What the man is doing? So many people, creating their own small dramas, their own Hollywood endings. What difference? Cars scurrying by like so many ants rushing to the queen, a seething crowd listening en masse to weather warnings of black ice, accident reports, tuneless songs sung too loudly over a dismal drum beat.

She despises them.

Her dislike of most people has become a blind spot she does not bother to examine any more.

From downstairs she can hear the hum of the twins practising their violins. They are a strange twosome, always together, indisputably identical. That isn't what makes them strange, of course, it is something more, something impossible to pinpoint. They wrap themselves in their music as though in a thick armour that protects them from everyone, from everything. Their songs wind out the window and twirl around the old house on its sagging foundations at all hours of the day and night. When the girl climbs the stairs to her own apartment, she can see in their window two identical blond heads bowing over the violins as if in prayer. What do they pray for, she wonders, what are they hiding from? They would tell Harry, if he asked. They idolize Harry. But she doesn't want to think about him now, she can't think about him now, the miles of green salty ocean between them buffer her from him. He can't reach her from where he is. She is almost free of Harry, but for the tremulous whine of the violins reaching for her from downstairs.

In the attic window of the house next door, a fat, orange-striped tabby stares back at her; the green marbles of his eyes flash as cars rush downhill, first towards them, then past. Hurrying.

Waiting.

The man gets into his truck, dressed as he would be for the meeting he lied and said he was attending. He lies so easily, he is almost totally unnerved. Has to pause in the driveway and look long and hard at the lighted windows in his home, has to drag himself away, ultimately aware of the first stitch of guilt in what will somehow grow into a tapestry.

Drive away.

He drives away from his family, passing on the way the still-lit greenhouses where the few workers who stay on during the winter work inside in the hot dampness, music blasting from stereos so loudly the glass itself rattles. These men nurture the seedlings that one day will be tall enough to sell, to be dug from the earth, lifted by crane into waiting trucks and transported to golf courses and nurseries and homes around the city. Eventually, they will tower overhead, a hundred years from now, and they will stand strong through seasons of blistering heat and blasting storms, roots dug deep and woven in a steel web through the earth itself. Long after he is gone.

So what does it matter?

He turns left at the bottom of the driveway, and does not glance back to his home again.

Is home the same as family?

The girl has no family to speak of, a sister far away in some midwestern state she struggles to name, but cannot. Idaho. Iowa. Ohio. The girl is at home now, the place where she sleeps, where she works, where she lives.

Home is where you hang your hat.

Home:

A one-bedroom apartment perched precariously at the uppermost reaches of a rambling house, a house that sounds like ghosts and history and the passing of families. The apartment is on Faithful Street. The girl admires irony, bathes in it, tastes it on her tongue, speaks the words aloud and listens to them snapping in the empty room. Faithful. Street.

Boys and girls come out to play
The moon doth shine as bright as day
Leave your supper and leave your sleep
And join your playfellows in the street.

An ancient rhyme, unforgotten, drifts from her lips in a murmur. Did she speak? There is no one there to listen, to hear.

The floors creak at intervals although the girl is not moving. The house is settling downwards, sinking towards the heart of the damp basement three stories below where coin-driven laundry machines hum and rattle, lulled by the mewling of the violins. Slowly, over a hundred years, the house decays, noisily — board by board, nail by nail — only to be resurrected, with fresh paint, some new windows, by new owners with new hopes to rebuild and repair.

A clock ticks slowly at the end of the hall, minutes slide haltingly forward with the jerk of the long hand. Hours play strange games, slipping by with quicksilver speed, hovering, slowing, waiting.

The cat stares in, unperturbed.

The window is open and violin scales accompany the air that occasionally jumps into the room and lifts the long white curtains, then lazily drops them back down to the cracked wood floors. Bridal veils cover so many innocent eyes. The man is married. The girl is twenty-three years old, and waiting, wrapped in a thin, cottony robe of white. A not-so-virginal sacrifice.

She is too nervous to be cold. Her fingers play up and down the arms of the couch. She rubs the nap one way, then the other. Traces circles on the cloth. Too nervous.

A sudden night descends, the dusk sinking away into the quicksand of darkness. Shadow and light play off each other, off every surface, each detail illuminated like a perfectly clear black-and-white photograph. When she inhales she smells the purity of her bleached surroundings, the slightly smoky echo of old fires from the tiny fireplace, the wax and carbon smell of the burned candles she uses to avoid the harshness of the bare bulbs.

Interested?

Against the milky monotony of the backdrop are the following:

An antique bed, posts carved with the grimaces of peculiar gargoyles;

A cracked bathtub, it's claws resting on perfectly polished brass eggs, the detail of the talons visible from the doorway; four sculptures on the mantel, crudely shiny black lumps of clay.

The eye can spin around the white room, barely able to distinguish the white wall from the white sofa, the white mantel, the white rugs. White table. The travelling eye can rest on each of these objects in turn, or ignore them, remain dazzled by the ephemeral white. Bed. Bathtub. Art.

Wait — examine the art more closely:

The sculptures are much more than crude, shiny lumps of clay. These statues have voices, they scream at the girl. They are memories that ricochet around her mind like gunfire. She can shut them out if she tries hard enough, drown them out with every ounce of strength she carries in her tiny, muscled body. Sometimes she lets them take her. A surrender.

From time to time, she wonders if it happened at all — there were no witnesses. There never are. Dreams and reality occasionally merge in memory into some middle ground where what is true and what is imagined are the same thing.

When she was young, she believed in fairies. Angels. As soon as she turned thirteen, she realized it was all a dream and put them out of her mind.

Now, celebrities spill their tales of incest, rape, sodomy on the afternoon talk shows. Appalling visions dripping from their perfectly capped smiling teeth, making the truths seem glamorous, forgivable. Did this happen to them, or to her? Angels, real? Or imagined?

Walk carefully towards the past. Touch the statues. The fist of fear punches through to her spine, twists her stomach in a serpent's impossible dance, plays its pathetic meaningless movie out against the darkened red of her closed eyelids. Not now, she whispers to her phantoms, not tonight.

Phantoms, real? Or imagined?

She was twelve years old.

She is twelve years old. Twelve. Posing stock still in the cold studio, she watches the artist working and reworking her body into the slimy wet earth. She grinds her teeth together to keep them from chattering, reminding herself that this is art, and that art is good. Her skin has been crusted over with drying grey marks from his probing fingers. She wonders if she will be able to wash them off, she imagines him spreading the clay over her body more and more heavily until she is encased in it completely. This is Art, and Art is good. She tries not to flinch as his filthy wet fingers probe inside, slide down to rearrange her legs and arms, tilting a shoulder, moving some hair. She thinks of the art teacher's wife, frowns as she tries to remember the woman's name. Don't scowl, he says, you'll ruin everything. He slaps her, unexpectedly, a sudden flicker of rage dancing across his clean-shaven cheek, stopping in his ice-grey eyes. You have to be still, he says. He forces her to stand. He pushes himself into her.

Does he really?

Be good, her mother told her, do as your teachers tell you. (Is this what she meant? If this is good, why does it feel so bad?)

She'll be a good girl, her father said. She's always been a good girl. (Always a good girl, Daddy.)

Matilda, the good girl says out loud, smiling. That is the name of his wife. Matilda. The word spasms against the sloppy pastels taped loosely to the grey brick walls, reverberating in the emptiness. The papers seem to flap in an unseen wind. Matilda, she says louder, shouting. Matilda. The word is a scream, a sob.

You. Little. Bitch, he says slowly, and slaps her again.

The girl-child drifts away from the scene, watching his violent organ whither as he shoves it back into his pants, cages it behind the metal teeth of his zipper.

He gives her the statues.

They're ugly, anyway, he says, his words stinging more sharply than his hands. You are an ugly little slut. I don't know why I wasted my time. These are yours now, they all belong to you.

She is sorry. Sorry, sorry, she mumbles through her tears. Sorry.

Afterwards, she goes back to her room and stands for hours under the scalding hot shower, ignoring the knocks of the other girls on the door. Hurry up, they shout, we all need a turn. You're taking too long. Go away, she whispers. Go away. The hot steam rises around her, slowly lifting off the layers of clay, the grime swirling endlessly down the drain.

Days later, in art class, she glazes the figures herself, long-legged, pubescent figurines. Layers and layers of dull black that turn glossy in the hellfire of the kiln. Layers so thick they disguise the details of the face, the navel, the crease at the top of the leg, the sharp points of the nipple. Again and again, she adds layers. Sacrifices the girls into the punishing oven.

Heat. Fire.

She wants to put her hands in too, watch the flesh melt into a shiny scar.

Art. Art is good.

Real, or imagined?

After all, she was only twelve. She still believed in fairies. And angels.

Rape. Is this her excuse for infidelity? Don't be naive. It is only part of the patchwork quilt that makes up a life. A square of colour no bigger or smaller or brighter than another, attached by a single thread. The girl holds her head high, her back straight, as she sits. She is proud, this young girl. She makes no excuses.

She pushes the memory away and replaces it with a happier one:

A tent in the woods behind the house, snuggled up against her sister's back, cookies stolen from the kitchen reduced to a few crumbs on a paper plate. Smell the stale plastic walls. Breathe deeply from the tiny screened window, the fresh summer air is freedom. Tell me another story, she says, tell me one more before we go to sleep. How warm it was inside that tent, one summer. How peaceful. Her sister lay back on the sleeping bag and lit another cigarette. Only if you don't tell Mom I was smoking, she whispers, I'll tell you a really scary one.

Outside, the freezing rain drips down from the eaves like an irregular pulse. Rapid, then slow. Loud, then barely audible. She sits on the couch, staring into the fire, listening. She presses her finger against her wrist and counts out the beats of her heart.

There is a knock on the door.

A moment of paralysing fear, self doubt, and the shocked realization that she has forgotten to get dressed.

She waits for another knock, more urgent, repeated.

She lets the man stand outside, knocking, picturing him dripping wet at the outside door, his gentle suede coat spattered with dark water stains, moisture beading in his carefully sprayed hair. Does he stop and listen to the violins? Can he hear the music?

Knock.

She opens the door and the room fills with his life, with his colour, with his smells, as though what was black-and-white before has been retouched with colour so bright it can only be a dream. They both take a step forward, then back again, the air is thick and soup-like with sex and desire. An awkward hesitation as each drinks the other in warily from opposite sides of the door-sill before they reach out, she touches his sleeve, he brushes his thumb along her cheek, catches his fingers in a curl.

Both are speechless, there is nothing to say. They have been talking for months, forever.

Now is the time for touching.

Now is the winter of our discontent.

The girl steps aside in the narrow hallway.

The door closes behind the man, solidly fitting into its frame with a sound of finality, the latch dropping easily into place.

They sink into the affair as though it were a goose-down quilt of unbearable softness, a thick warmth that can envelope them so completely that they all but disappear into the feathers.

Wait:

To end it here would be too simple. Look more closely. See the way he reaches into her robe and cups her breast, kissing her nipple so gently she can hardly feel his lips, his tongue. See how she cradles his head in her arms, her hands running through his grey-brown hair, feeling his scalp with the gentle caress of a mother. They sink into each other, like a meeting of sand and water, sliding into one another like the tide. Eyes wide open, they understand that something important has begun, a change in the volcanic bubbling core of their beings.

They are terrified.

They are thrilled.

Watch:

The way he traces the outline of her vertebrae with his mouth, probing. Follows the pattern of the black-brown freckles. How her back arches towards him, her hair falling down over his face. See him drinking in the sight of her, her skin so white. So white.

See how they part like the guilty, like criminals: eyes turned inwards into their souls, secretly delighted, outwardly chastened.

As the girl falls asleep she dreams of the shadow tattoos that fell over his back in the moonlight, breathes so deeply of his scent on the pillow that she becomes dizzy and for the first time in twenty-three years senses something that might be joy coursing through her veins, as sure and silent and rhythmic as her blood.

Happy birthday, she whispers.

The man drives away. God, he says, his own voice startling in the silence of the truck cab. Oh my God.

Did this happen?

The moon hangs in the sky like a paper plate, comically huge and white, surrounded by a halo of cold. The rain has stopped. When? The night is perfectly still and silent, traffic does not exist. The wet roads have frozen in place, in time, in a shadow of ice on the pavement. He is alone in his truck, inching slowly towards home.

He turns around.

A U-turn.

Dangerous on such hidden ice, black as death. He circles the block to stare up at her darkened window.

The wife falls asleep counting stitches. Knit one, purl one. Drop a stitch or two.

The damage is already done.

CHAPTER 2

The man wakes up before sunrise; the moon shining in through the skylight illuminates the sleeping body of his wife like guilt. Snores escape her half-open mouth. Does she snore? He sits up — drags the sheets and blankets with him, aware of their texture against his skin, damp cotton warmth — causing her to roll towards him. He can feel the heat of her body pressing against his leg.

Time is it? Her voice heavy with sleep.

Early, he answers, pushing the blankets away. It's too early.

She sighs and turns over, pulling the blankets and bedspread and quilt so that they are half falling off onto the floor on her side of the bed. He sits there for a moment longer, just watching, a trail of goosebumps rising on his flesh in the chill of the room.

When was the last time he made love to his wife?

She sleeps in an old T-shirt from a holiday taken in Mexico, the parrots and palm trees long ago faded almost to white. Under the shirt her breasts flop listlessly to one side.

He takes the time to press a kiss onto her forehead, smells the thick scent of dreams and sweat and moisturizer.

Her hand reaches up and pushes him away.

The greenhouses are deserted. He labours in the dark — seed

the trays, fertilize, water, test the moisture in the soil. Still in darkness, he goes into the smaller building where he grows trees and flowers, crossbreeding them, experimenting. It's a hobby, he tells people. That's all.

His heart thuds loudly in his chest.

It is hot and bright in the room, to try to force the blooms. Artificial daylight. An artificial season. An artificial climate.

Nothing is real any more. It is all a dream.

He records his progress methodically in hardbound notebooks: the beginning of a bud, a flower that has wilted and died. He works until the sun begins to come up, then he stops. Sits there and watches the orange orb struggle above the treetops inch by inch.

It is a perfectly clear winter day.

Yesterday's rain has been blown away and forgotten.

It is so cold in the apartment that the girl finds that the water she left in a glass by the bed has iced over. The heater must be broken again. What does it matter? Cold or hot. She thinks of the man, stretches until her legs cramp up with charley horses, smiles. Her breaths puff and dangle in front of her lips. Frozen happiness.

Will he call?

Of course.

When?

Later.

What will she do?

She must work, obviously.

Work is the easiest distraction.

Out the window, she can see the pale blue sky, so pale it appears that a dome of ice has formed between the city and the real sky, turquoise-blue and hot.

Work.

In two different parts of the city, man and girl stare at the telephone as though it has magic powers that it is choosing to withhold.

The wife sleeps late, until the roar of the furnace brings the house to a more palatable temperature, and shivers in her empty bed. The day stretches before her, endless.

Sometimes, she does not want to bother to get up.

There are birds at the bird-feeder outside the window, diving towards the glass and then turning away at the very last moment, hovering on the edge of the tray to win a few seeds, an extra moment of survival, before being knocked away by the wings of another.

She thinks of the things she needs to do around the house: vacuum the thick rugs, scrub the bathroom, maybe make a stew or some soup to freeze. Christmas is coming — she should bring the boxes of decorations down from the attic and begin weaving the lengths of red and green garland through the balcony, across the mantel. Polish the silver, used only at Christmas — the hand-beaten bowl, the elaborate trays, the cutlery.

She gets up.

Shower, dress, make the bed.

So much to do, to get ready for Christmas.

When the phone rings, jangling in six rooms of the house, it is a relief really, to be called away.

Mom ...

So much like when they were small, calling in the dark. MOM! MOM! I've had a bad dream! I need a drink of water! I'm sick! MOM!

Mom ...

Now it is her son, her grown son, her baby, Derek.

Mom, can you come over?

Of course.

The children always come first.

The sun shines down on the miles of trees, short and tall, some getting too big to sell, so tall they will soon be immovable, will become permanent parts of the landscape. The miles of trees in winter, they could make a person crazy or, at the very least, dizzy. Rows and rows of leafless trees. Like a graveyard. She cannot see her husband, but knows he is there somewhere, pacing the long rows like an expectant father, waiting for the rebirth of spring.

She finds him standing amongst the exotic pines, their trunks bent and twisted like arthritic joints. Like little old men, gnarled feet trapped in the freezing soil, buckling in the wind.

I'm going to see Derek. Her voice is loud and alarming. A flock of chickadees rises and then settles back into a nearby holly bush.

Oh?

Yes. He called, he seemed upset.

Drive carefully.

I guess you don't want to come. Don't you want to know what's wrong?

No.

Maybe you'll come with me someday.

Maybe. Don't count on it.

How can the man be so cold towards his own son?

You should be kinder, the wife whispers into the wind as she trudges through the snow to her car. You should be nicer.

The man does not love his son, because his son doesn't love women. What could be more simple than that?

For every action there is an equal and opposite reaction.

The girl sits down at her desk to write, picks up her pen, squints down at the blank yellow paper. The words do not come. Instead, she is thinking about how gentle the man was when he entered her for the first time. The difference in the texture of his leathery skin, versus Harry's smooth hairless chest. Harry, who is a million miles away. A thousand miles. An ocean, a country, a culture away. A year away, in the past. She breathes deeply and allows her lungs to push out all thoughts of Harry. A thought to be reserved for later. For now, there is only last night: her mind's eye skims the man's body, slightly paunchy but otherwise firm, lines of muscle visible on arms and chest. In fact, the grey chest hairs are the only visible sign of age. Grey chest hairs. She breathes deeply again, to force herself back to her centre, the desk tilting slightly before her. Frowning, she forces her pen to paper. Work.

There is nothing in her mind, except the man. He has expanded to fill all the spaces.

Perhaps there is nothing left for her to write. Her pen makes doodles on the paper, loops and swirls. Schoolgirl hearts.

How did they meet — the girl who writes, the man who grows trees?

Listen:

It is May. The day is cloudy, with sunny intervals of a warmth that sinks into the joints like a sweater or cup of hot tea. Soon it will be summer.

The girl is working.

She has been asked to write a piece about experimental species of trees that are grown to produce medicines that are beneficial in fighting cancer. Curing cancer. Could this be true? A cure, so much hope. The girl works exclusively for a few magazines, writing scientific facts into stories of future possibilities. So she is consulting the requisite expert, filling in occasional sentences that she knows he is going to say. She has read about his experiments in growing trees, his accidental contribution to science. She knows all that he knows, she thinks, the story is all but complete. Still, she must make the journey out to his farm, ask the questions, get the answers. A part of her job she both loves and hates: the writing itself holds no surprises, but she has no control over the people that she meets.

She goes to his greenhouses, where she is directed to his office by a stocky young boy, who seems to be dressed all in dirt, with some clothes underneath.

She expects to see a tall, stoop-shouldered old man, smelling of soil and manual labour and probably stale cigarette smoke. She has assumed his office will be an oversized closet, perhaps in his house, paperwork spread everywhere, coffee cups with moulding creamy brown liquid swirling in the murky depths. She thinks he will tell her nothing she does not already know, but that she will write down what he says dutifully, try to pry some catchy quotes out of him, knock off the article in a couple of hours. She does not plan to stay long.

Pushing open the office door, she sees immediately that she is completely wrong. His office is large, but lacks furnishings. His desk is an old dining table. There are no papers anywhere, closed bookshelves line the walls. At least a dozen lush green plants are arranged in front of a large plate glass window that overlooks the valley in the centre of the farm. The room smells green, and of moist dirt. There are pictures leaning up against the walls, not hung, just tossed in piles, half covered — amateur but beautiful oils, acrylics and watercolours featuring feathery apparitions interposed with thick rich forests, exotic (if twisted and distorted) houses and buildings. The girl does not normally like art of any kind, but she knows that these are good. She makes a note to herself to enquire after the artist, perhaps there is another story here.

The man comes into the room and takes her breath away.

No, that is not quite right.

The man comes into the room and she is immediately nervous and awkward. He is not what she expected, and she feels a childish heat crawling up her neck, over her cheeks. Her breath seems to be not quite forming from the base of her lungs. Short, fish-like puffs rise to her lips as though they have become gills and she is suddenly aware she is no longer under water. She flops around, gasping. She thinks he cannot tell, but feels as though she might faint, swoon like the heroine in a historical novel.

He is neither astoundingly good looking, nor gaunt and hoary as she had imagined. She finds it hard to speak, there is something in her mind stopping the words from forming correctly on her tongue. She is staring at his eyes, hazel. One fleck of darker brown. Outwards from the eyes, the wrinkles of one who smiles not with his mouth, but with his whole face. The nose not small, nor large. The lips, she wants, crazily, to reach forward and kiss.

Why? What makes them special?

Nothing. There is nothing extraordinary about him except the effect he is having on her.

What of the man, then? What does he see? A girl, attractively dressed. She has long dark curls springing free from a braid that hangs part way down her back. Her hair looks soft and pliable and he wants maybe to reach forward and touch it, that's all. He sees the circles under her eyes, the cheekbones that are just slightly too sharp. Chocolate-brown freckles too much of a contrast on her pale white skin. His gaze drops down, takes in the protruding collarbone, the hidden curves. She is too thin, and looks tired. He thinks of all the anorexic teenagers that filled the house when his own children were growing up.

He thinks of his wife, with her full, fleshy folds of skin.

He thinks, how long will this take. I need a cup of coffee. I have work to do.

He thinks, I wish I were younger and could seduce this girl, see her long curly hair flowing down her naked back. Freckled, white skin. Firm, with no flab.

He thinks about how long it has been since he has touched his wife.

The girl is speaking to him. She is mentioning the pictures on the wall.

My wife, he says. These are the first words that the man speaks to the girl. How ironic!

My wife is an artist, of sorts. Her gallery. He motions with his wrist.

The girl stares at his hand, short square nails at the end of solid fingers, callused, masculine in some ancient way. His wrists are stocky, with a sprinkling of dark hair crawling out of his sleeve, down onto the veins that pulse over the backs of his hands.

His wife.

She carefully assesses the weight he has put into this word. Wife. He has spoken so softly, she almost didn't catch the tone. What? she says, despite herself.

My wife.

This time the words are more solid, but do not ring heavily with love. She feels relieved.

The girl makes a note with a fine black pen on her pad of recycled yellow paper. Mrs. Tree, she writes, artist.

The small talk that they make seems to hang suspended above their heads in balloons, a cartoon language.

The girl knows she must steer the conversation towards the topic of her article, but she doesn't want to. The room is suffused in the warmth of mutual attraction and the smell of the greenery. She is afraid that the feeling will be punctured if he speaks of his trees, which she may be, at worst, bored by — after all, she probably knows as much of this topic as he.

The trees.

Ah, of course.

I suppose they will be a good business for you.

Good business, yes. I suppose.

So?

It's really a hobby. I mean, some types of trees take an awfully long time to grow. They have the potential to live for ever, but people are doomed to die long before the trees here are big enough or prolific enough to be beneficial.

The trees have the potential to give life.

Or just prolong misery.

There is always hope.

Ah. Yes. Hope. Let me show you the trees that are causing all the excitement.

He leads her into another greenhouse. His hand is on her elbow to guide her. Tiny shocks brush her skin. Almost imperceptible, did it really happen?

Do they both know?

Their heads are drawn together, like a magnet. He is speaking almost directly into her ear, and his proximity makes her immediately forget everything he is saying. She is aware of the heat of his words on her skin. He is aware of her skin.

Oh, so aware.

He shows her the trees.

They are four inches high.

These ones have been growing for a year, he says quietly. Write about that.

The girl mentally rewrites the article mentioning only a few of the things he said. Things other people have said. She will go back to the University Hospital and speak to an oncologist she knows there, take a different angle. There is nothing here. But still, she does not want to leave.

She begins to ask more questions, with a tentativeness that makes her seem, to him, to be a beginner. He asks how long she has been doing this.

Five years, she says. I'm sorry. I am not myself.

Oh, he says. All right. He feels confused.

The girl leaves in a flurry of paper. The man feels a headache beginning at the base of his skull.

For months, she works on the article, calling him to ask questions.

Calling him.

They talk often.

About trees?

No.

They talk often, about themselves. They turn each other into something that each is not: a necessary evil. They make each other necessary.

Months pass.

The girl loses the article to a writer who manages to meet deadlines. She writes stories about hairstyles for fashion magazines and has a hard time selling them in the unfamiliar market that is tough to break. She calls the editors at the science magazines where she works regularly, and explains she is taking some time off. I'm thinking of writing a book, she says. Aren't we all, says her favourite editor. Isn't everyone, replies another.

Her days empty out.

The man and the girl speak on the phone every day.

The doorbell rings and breaks the silence. The girl, startled, stares down at the yellow paper now filled with inky whirls and swirls. She has done nothing. No words, only drawings like embroidery filling up page after page. Nothing.

The doorbell rings, dragging the girl back to the present. A harsh buzz scraping at the stillness inside the room.

She wonders why the man did not ring last night. Instead, he knocked and knocked. She smiles.

The doorbell rings.

Yes?

It is her neighbour from downstairs with her curly-haired four-year-old, a sparkling diamond of a child. The neighbour, Alice, is a stripper. Gyrating around metal poles on mirrored stages to put peanut butter on her daughter's bread. Her wig today is blonde, and hangs in a straight white curtain down her back. Despite the fact her job is sordid, at best, she is startling beautiful. Kohl rings around fake blue eyes.

Yes?

I'm sorry, I hate to ask ...

Yes.

An excuse. She will take the child for the day. She will not have to work. Tomorrow, she promises herself, tomorrow. The child reaches up and takes her hand, dark brown eyes glinting with mischief.

Do you want to play?

Boys and girls come out and play.

Yes.

The door closes neatly, a promise is extended — only until six.

The girl becomes a babysitter.

Let's play.

The man walks away from the pines towards the greenhouse, suddenly cold and needing to be suffused in the warmth, the moist wet heat. Something deep in his leg is aching and he is suddenly afraid. Arthritis, he thinks, I'm getting old.

When the man's wife left, she kissed him goodbye. Perfunctory. He barely felt her lips on his, hardly noticed the fragrance that he used to love, the heady scent of Chanel and soap and hairspray and makeup. He patted her behind as she walked away, and looked up at the clear cold sky.

Dazed. He is in a daze. Fifty-two years old, in a daze over a woman, a girl well under half his age, in fact, a girl younger than his own daughter.

Breathe.

Breathe again.

Green air saturates his lungs. The dripping of the intricate maze of sprinklers goes unnoticed. He plunges his fingers into the soil in the seed trays, starting to plant spring bulbs to force into bloom early to sell at the flower stand at the foot of the drive. Feels the grit behind his nails, the cool damp give of the earth, thinks of the girl, astride, head tipped back as though she is falling. Towards or away? Falling just out of his grasp.

He tastes the girl's name on his tongue. Whispers to himself. A crush. A boy at the other end of the room is tinkering with the taps — he raises his eyes to look at the man. Something passes between them. The man feels the pulsating joy of youth.

The telephone is a magnet drawing him closer. He will not call yet, he will fight this, he will wait. The girl will wait.

An uninvited image of his wife on their wedding day: nineteen years old, skin smooth as marble. Dressed in a tower of white, elaborately frilly. She looks like a frosted cake, her eyes glimmer with tears as they say their vows. Tears of joy? Or for the hurt that was to come? How many times has he broken her heart?

He feels sick. Then and now. Nausea plunders his gut. Pictures of his mistresses of the past thirty years pass by like a slide show. None of them mattering. What is it about this girl that is different?

He is not so naive to think she will love him back with such intensity, she is too young, so young. A child, really. Perhaps that is what sets her apart. Sweet youth.

The girl is at home.

Do you want to play?

They make their way down the slippery stairs, bundled up to keep the ice from their warm inner cores. The child looks up. Her hands fly as she speaks, imitating Harry.

(Go away, Harry, the girl whispers inside her head. Leave me alone.)

In winter, my heart is made of snow.

Oh?

Yes, in spring it melts.

What happens then?

Then it makes a flower, silly.

Ah. Lucy.

Skipping down the sidewalk, Lucy trips and falls on tightly swathed knees, bounces back up again like a prizefighter.

Ooops.

I'm not even going to cry, she says with great importance. Even though it hurts. A lot.

The girl laughs, carries the blankety bundle of warm child all the way to the bus stop, having to be careful herself so as not to slip and drop all that fragile happiness onto the cold, brittle cement. She thinks of the man, allows herself to think of this child as hers. Hers and his. She can see the three of them walking down the road hand in hand. Then, unbidden, another image. The child is eighteen, graduating high school. The man is sixty-seven.

How old is sixty-seven? Wheelchair old? Toothless old?

No.

But too old, for an eighteen-year-old child.

This is not their child. This is Lucy, daughter of the beautiful Alice. The sordid Alice.

Stepping onto the warm, befogged bus, a flicker — just a spattering — of doubt begins to nudge at the girl.

The clearness of the day has caused the temperature to plummet.

The wife, driving on the iced-glass roads, keeps her hands clenched firmly on the steering wheel. The radio is tuned to the CBC, classical music erupts from the tinny speakers. She forces herself to hum, thinks of her son in his rambling house always full of people and voices and food and laughter. She thinks of how much it would mean to her son to see his father, who does not visit, does not see his son, does not love this son because his heart is closed and cruel and knows only one way. His way. The drive requires all of her concentration, the small blue car slipping side to side on the busy roads. Why does no one else seem to be sliding? Only her little blue tin can, ricocheting around, barely keeping within the lines on her lane.

The man caves in to the demand of the phone. He dials, two times. Three times, before he can get the number right. The phone rings, echoes in the vacant apartment. He listens to the recorded empty voice of the girl and thinks maybe he does not have to see her again, maybe that is all there was, one night.

He can laugh at himself in the privacy of his office, surrounded by paintings done by his wife. He will keep calling until he reaches her, he will be waiting at her apartment when she finally comes home.

The mailman drops a letter through the slot on the girl's front door. It too finds an empty apartment, slips through the slot to drift down onto the floor. Lies face down, fancy stamps staring into the small, square mat.

The girl and the child spend the day wandering through the park in the frigid cold. Lucy is captivated by the empty swing sets, the slide that will not let her go: the frost has made a sticky slope. She sits at the top and laughs and laughs until the girl comes and helps her wiggle down the steel ramp. There is no one else in the world, save a couple of people walking their old dogs. No one else. They play until their cheeks glow bright red and the child begins to lose her fine temper. Begins to cry when she falls gently on to the grass.

Time to go home.

She can see the man sitting in his truck, the windows steamed up from the paper cup of coffee he holds in his hands. Her heart skips. He is here. Waiting for her. Watching? She frowns. Stalking?

No.

Only the man, waiting. She cannot stop herself from grinning, teeth gleaming white against the terrible grey blue of the winter day. Hurries the child up the stairs.

Knock.

Yes?

We're back, Alice.

Yes. Alice yawns. The makeup around her eyes is smeared, her wig removed to reveal mouse-brown hair scraped down against her scalp. Glasses slide down her nose.

Thanks.

Any time, Alice. Bye, Lucy.

The child disappears into the messy warmth of her mother's apartment, not even looking back at the girl.

There is nowhere to go but up the stairs. She trudges towards her own apartment, turns at the landing to beckon to the man.

Yes.

Opening the front door, her foot falls onto the letter with the fancy postage that she does not see. She is looking over her shoulder to see if the man is following.

Hi.

Missed you.

You too.

Here, let me. He helps her off with her bulky winter coat. Peeling down the layers of clothing, hands roaming and stroking.

Hi.

When he kisses her, she can taste stale coffee on his insistent tongue. Her stomach growls and roars, tumultuous with hunger. They make love standing in the front hallway, pants tight around their knees. No dignity. Somehow, in the middle of it all, the girl looks down and sees the damp envelope, kicks it under the hall table just as the man reaches his climax.

Well.

They move into the living room, light a fire.

Cold day.

Yes, but clear. We went to the park.

We?

Me and Lucy. She lives downstairs. She's four.

Ah.

How was your day?

My day? Fine. Just fine. I was thinking about you.

The girl falls in love with the way his voice breaks slightly, nervous. It is so easy.

You know I am much too old for you.

According to whom?

Well. I'm married.

I know.

You deserve better than me.

You don't want me to agree, do you?

No.

Then I won't. You are not old.

Old enough to be your father.

But you aren't my father.

No.

Is this all we will ever talk about?

No. Tell me about you.

There is nothing to tell, what you see is what you get!

I like what I see, come over here.

Touching is easier than talking. It is possible that the physical chemistry between two people can overwhelm their need to talk. When the girl touches the man, he swears he feels a current jump and spark in his veins. When the man touches the girl, she is finally warm.

Is this all we will ever talk about?

Harry reaches out to touch the girl, from across the Pacific, from all those miles away, the flowering stamps on the letter flicker angrily under the table in the hall.

The girl has already averted her gaze.

Chapter 3

Thursday mornings, the wife volunteers at the AIDS hospice — a nightmare world of youth, extinguished. Of fear and dying. Of death.

Why?

AIDS is her biggest fear, the terror that wakes her up at night, sheets soaked with sympathetic sweat. The fear lurks in her conviction that her son will get AIDS, that God will somehow punish him for his choice. That his father will be proven to be right — that his choice will kill him. She would never voice this fear, never let her son know that she feels this way. She understands that her son is careful, that these days everyone is careful, that "gay" does not equal "AIDS", but this does not ease her panic. She understands that her husband, her daughter, her next-door neighbour, everyone she knows, is at risk one way or another. But her heart beats out her fear every moment of Thursday morning.

I will help them, God, she prays. But don't take my son, my gentle son. My love, my life. I will help them.

There is never enough air on Thursdays. She drives with the windows open, freezing or sweltering depending on the season. Her hungry lungs pull and strain, but there isn't enough oxygen to fill her up.

On Thursdays, she smokes two whole packs of cigarettes. Light, reduced tar. Two whole packs fill up her ravenous lungs.

She drives to the hospital by a different route each week. She needs to see more each time. She cruises up and down suburban side streets, looks at houses, at lives, normal lives untouched by sickness. Each time she sees someone outside changing a Christmas bulb, or getting into their car, or walking a dog, she can let their normalcy comfort her. The sight of a car wobbling along, student-driver sign propped crookedly in the back window. A young mother perched on the lawn watching in amazement as her son sails down the street on a new sled. A snowman, melting. Everything is perfect and whole. It washes over her like a balm.

Inside the hospital, choking on the smell of antiseptic and sickness, she plasters a smile on her face, pops a strong peppermint in her mouth, and reminds herself that this could be her son.

Sometimes it is like walking into a concentration camp. The men are so thin and wasted — they have never eaten, they are skeletons waiting to die. They have always been dying. A litany of suffering.

There is another smell behind the cleaners and medicines. A starchy sweet smell. A smell of decay.

Occasionally, there are women on the ward, but not so many, not nearly as many women as men — young, creative, brilliant men, middle-aged angry men. Rich and poor, ugly and beautiful, brought together as though it was the end of the world.

Tirelessly, she listens to their stories, stories that seem desperate in the telling. Hear this story! Listen! Remember! It is all I have left ... my father beat me, my mother left me, my parents live so far away. I had a dog once. My lover left me. Let me tell you about the time I went camping with the Scouts. Let me tell you what my parents did when they found out. Let me tell you about my first love, my first car, my first time. Love me. Hold my hand. I am afraid to die.

Their voices are a chorus that rise in a hymn in her head, in her ears. In the car on the way home, she tries to drown it out with the CBC. But she can still hear it: I am not dying. I am not afraid to die. I will go softly into this good night. The drugs will work. Why won't my lover come and visit? Let me tell you about my T-cells. Let me ask you about AZT. Read this, there is hope for a cure. Tell me it will be all right. Tell me. Tell me.

A cacophony of real pain amidst health-care workers wearing rubber gloves, health-care workers chatting about their plans for dinner, a movie they saw, a book they read.

Some of the volunteers are HIV positive, the dreaded virus is not full-blown AIDS. Yet. They hover around the wards, marking the days until they will lie in the bed. Not me, they promise themselves, working a little harder. Breathing a little deeper.

Not me.

The wife makes sure she touches each patient on her ward. She hugs them and kisses their foreheads and holds their hands. She plays hours of gin rummy, cribbage, hearts. She reads out loud from books and magazines, laughs and tells jokes. She will be mother to all of them, she feeds off their love like a shark. Devours it. Their love will somehow protect her son.

She is not a saint, she is only bargaining with God. It is purely a business negotiation.

Sometimes, on the way home, she stops in a church. She listens to the sound of her flat shoes slapping against the cold, hard floor. Smells the dusty smell of bibles and prayers. Sometimes, she kneels on the hard wooden pew and prays. For her son. For forgiveness. For her family. For herself.

The stained-glass windows are so beautiful they bring tears to her eyes. The sheer beauty of the coloured glass is almost enough, almost enough to make her believe.

Oh, God. Jesus Christ. Hail Mary full of grace.

She does not know the words to all the prayers.

Our father who art in heaven ...

Walking out, she always feels disoriented. She is not religious, after all. An atheist since college — she doesn't belong here. That's what makes her prayers more powerful, that's what makes them count.

Can you make a bargain with a deity that does not exist?

Off to see the faggots then, her husband states.

Not faggots, dear.

Fairies, then.

Don't ...

Whatever.

They're sick.

Exactly.

You're impossible! Ignorant! They're dying ... they ...

Bye, dear.

On the phone, the plastic immutable connection, the umbilical cord that allows both girl and man to get through the endless hours between them, the man tells the girl about his faggot son, and his wife working at the hospital.

Fairies? Faggots? What kind of talk is that? I don't believe you, the girl says, choking on her shock. Don't be so stupid. That's so stupid ... I don't ...

Stupid?

A hollow silence.

Stupid?

You aren't stupid, but this ... I didn't know. How can you. How can you hate your own son?

Hate?

It sounds so awful, to hear you being so ... ignorant.

Whatever you say, dear.

Dear?

I miss you.

Me too.

Goodbye.

The girl phones him back.

Don't ever, she says, her voice shaking. Don't ever call me dear.

Oh.

Dear is for your wife. Not for me. Never for me.

Sorry. Really, I didn't think.

No, I'm sorry. Never mind.

Hanging up the phone the man's head falls into his hands. His neck feels stiff and tight, so much tension pulsing through his veins, flowing in and out of his lungs. Why?

Love, he whispers. Oh shit. What am I doing?

But then he remembers: how the girl cried the first time they made love, how her head tipped back and crystal tears rolled up over her forehead, disappearing into her mane of hair. Crystal tears.

The girl runs.

Takes the letter, folded carefully into her pocket, layers on the grey fleece, the gloves that wick moisture away from her body, the running shoes filthy and worn and stiff from stepping in mud and puddles. She runs to the deserted park, a hollow void of people, allows her mind to empty completely. She wonders why, when she is running, the man's name echoes through her head with every footstep. A chant. Bigot, she thinks furiously, but she has already begun to forgive him. Dear.

She doesn't know him at all.

Her feet thud against the path.

She doesn't know him, but she has to have him.

She doesn't know him, but she needs him.

She sits on a swing to read, the letter folded against her pounding heart. The swing is rubber. Her legs pinch together uncomfortably. To distract herself, she pushes off and lets herself rise up through the cold. Rises up, drops down, rises up, drops down, until her heart slows to normal. Until she cannot feel her legs trapped in the child-sized seat.

The letter is written on rice paper, so translucent that when she holds it up to the light the words form incomprehensible elaborate swirls on the paper. She sniffs, puppy-like, at the ink. Nothing.

Nothing.

Nothing, Harry, she whispers triumphant. Nothing, she shouts. Why not? The park is barren, devoid of life.

She reads. It is hard to hear the words over the sound of her breathing, over the sound of her spindly pulse.

His name is a scrawl and line across the bottom of the page. Harry. It takes up the whole page, saying everything, while the words themselves say nothing. His letter sounds like his voice, flat and hollow. He describes what he has seen. He tells her that the water is warm and bluer than at home, that the fish look strange. Alien. He speaks of night dives, where the colours become more vivid, unstained by the sunlight that washes away the truth. He tells her that he cannot read lips in other languages, but bodies all speak the same way. He is getting by just fine. Without her, she supposes, getting along fine without you is what he means.

The letter is hard to understand. It might say: will you wait for me? Or else it says: I have moved on, I'm over you.

It's hard to tell.

You can only really understand Harry if you see his hands flying as he talks, if you can feel his hands touching you, his eyes touching you, as he speaks in his empty noteless voice. The girl reads and rereads the letter. A crow calls out from the top of a brittle tree. An elderly man smoking a pipe walks by, frowning. A poodle in a sweater trails listlessly at his heels. In the resounding emptiness, both man and dog look like extras on a movie set. She laughs out loud, only it sounds more like a cough.

A pinprick of rain hits her cheek. A drop of rain.

Wait:

Maybe it is a tear.

The girl cries silently for a full minute. She throws the letter into the bin where dog walkers discard Baggies of excrement. She can barely remember what Harry looks like, this boy who thinks he owns her. He has been gone for months, walking out of her life through the airport security, back straight and proud, black hair cascading down his back like Pocahontas. She watched him go and felt relief.

Relief? No.

She watched him go and felt afraid. No, that is not right either. She did not even watch him go.

How can she wait for this person she does not even remember?

You're breathing too fast, Harry gestures impatiently. You'll run out of air.

Don't, she shakes her head at him underwater. I'm not.

You are, he says. You're going to run out.

Harry's hands flow more smoothly in water than on land. He becomes more graceful. More elegant.

She tries to make her body move like his, feeling the tug of the current against her flippers. She passed the course without any problem. Got the certification. Only with Harry do her lungs get tight and empty. She tries to relax, to look around, find the things he has told her about so lovingly. So tenderly.

She looks up at the surface, seeing only how far away it is, how far they are sinking. He gestures one way and another and she follows his hands desperately, seeing nothing but endless bottle-green darkness sliced through with ribbons of light, knife blades of sunlight. She breathes deeper against the regulator. Her lungs feel tight. A band of tension creeps around her chest.

He points.

Nothing. Nothing, Harry, she thinks. There is nothing there.

The water is stifling.

They are in the shallows. Harry stands on the sea floor, the tiny fronds of seaweed waving around his feet like a lawn, an ordinary green lawn, moving in a slow-motion wind. His hair floats around his head in an enormous cloud, swaying with the reeds. He looks around, his hands smoothly moving from one word, one thought, to the next. She can't keep up, and eventually she stops trying.

She doesn't have enough air. She taps her tank and points to the surface.

There is a gesture, in sign language, that means I told you so. The girl pushes towards the rippling ceiling, not looking, rising slowly sunwards.

Still standing on the bottom, Harry looks once more into the thick kelp. Then he sees it, the dart of a tail. The familiar square nose. Tiny, but still — a shark. Mud shark.

Smiling, he kicks his feet, follows the slim black figure of the girl up to the surface.

Afterwards, she is angry with him.

I don't know why you're mad at me, he says. I told you not to breathe so hard.

She doesn't say anything. Why bother?

That's Harry. Harry is always right.

A single snowflake drifts past her face. She remembers that it is cold.

She goes over to the garbage and retrieves the crumpled letter, flattening it against her muscular thigh. Flattening it, then crumpling it again, running away before she can change her mind.

She thinks about skin. How soft it can be. How sensitive. Her feet pound rhythmically on the frozen grass, her joints slowly thaw with every step.

The man is chopping wood behind the house, arms swinging in perfect arcs, the heavy axe head cracking down on each massive stump. Laying the axe down carefully, blade pointing in, he goes inside to call his travel agent. Books another ticket on the flight he must take tomorrow, a ticket that costs ten times as much as the original.

He argues with the agent, on principle, because this is ridiculous. The woman sighs heavily, her voice crackling with irritation. Hostility. Do you want the ticket or not?

He would have paid anything, money drifting away in the tide of his feelings. What does it matter? He buys the girl a ticket to California.

Yes.

No.

Wait — his wife pays the bills, will see two tickets on his credit card statement. He will be caught, and will have to confess. What will happen?

He calls the travel agent back, says to hold the ticket, he will come in and pay cash.

Cash?

Yes.

A knowing silence, the woman is an agent of many small infidelities. She can read the signs.

Ah. Fine. She cannot keep the victory out of her tone, and hangs up, wondering why she feels like she has won.

He slips the ticket into the girl's mailbox on his way back home.

Mailboxes are a thoroughfare for expectations and desires encapsulated in regulation sized envelopes. Some stamps are more threatening than others. Some envelopes bear no stamps at all.

The moonrise seems to come earlier every day. The man pauses on the stairs, listening to the haunting melody of violins, staring at the ephemeral moon rising into the clouds. The thick, suffocating clouds. Look at him standing there, between the girl and the wife, trapped in the musical strings. His face is upturned towards the light, as though it could be a source of warmth, like the sun.

The man does not notice when the music stops, his eyes are half shut when he hears the voices.

Look, they say together. Are you all right?

He opens his eyes to the twins. They hover in front of him, slippered feet shuffling on the icy stair.

Are you visiting? asks one.

Are you looking for someone? asks the other.

The man says nothing. Behind the boys, the moon is suspended between cloud and earth. It illuminates their hair, making them look almost holy. Like angels.

Look, they say again, exchanging glances. Are you lost? Do

you need help?

The man shakes his head.

Look, he says, pointing behind them at the moon disappearing into the darkness. When they turn to see, he speaks again so low they can hardly hear. It was so beautiful, with the music.

Does he?

His hands reach out and land on the right shoulder of one, the left of the other. For a second, he stands there, his hands resting like feathers. He can feel the warmth of their skin through their thin blue T-shirts. He can feel the bone of their shoulder, pressing up through the skin like the wings of birds. Pushing past them, he almost slips on the stairs. Almost loses his grip on the icy balcony. In his mind he tumbles head over heels.

He pushes past the twins, without a word.

No, that isn't right.

He pushes past the twins and they say, are you sure we can't help you? We think you must be lost.

And the man says, no, I'm not. And strides away into the burgeoning darkness.

The twins stand motionless, their bare feet melting patches in the ice. They watch the moon as it disappears.

Strange, they say at the same time. He looked lost.

One reaches out and brushes one blond hair off the other's forehead, tenderly. Lovingly. The brothers go back inside and settle on their identical stools. In perfect sync, their hands reach out for the violins.

Derek is preparing dinner for his lover, actually microwaving yesterday's meal. The heavy spoon bangs against the inside of the casserole as he vehemently scoops a ridiculously large serving onto a delicate plate.

The plate came from an auction. White china with hand-painted butterflies. Tiny, but so detailed that when he first saw it, it took his breath away. Beautiful. He wants to drop it on the floor and watch it disintegrate into a pile of powdered bone.

His lover is watching hockey in the living room with his feet on the coffee table, allowing the sickly stench of sweat to mingle with the fresh cut flowers arranged in the crystal bowl.

It's quite a scene. Is it familiar?

The son thinks of all the times his mother said to his father:

Get your feet off the table.

Come and eat in the kitchen,

I will not wait on you like a galley slave.

The son wants to say these words to his lover, but he does not. He allows them to curdle in his throat, to be swallowed down like bile. The TV vibrates as the crowd roars. He carries the reheated curry into the living room and places it in front of the other man like an offering. His hands reach out unbidden and begin massaging the other man's neck as his head moves back and forth, following the small puck on the ice.

His lover does not even look at his food, shoving it into his mouth as though he were doing it a favour. He belches noisily.

A-minor, says Derek, out of habit.

His lover shoots him a withering glance. A glance made of hate and resentment and blades and ice winds. A small voice in Derek's head is whispering, chanting. He's leaving, it says. He's already gone.

Derek gets down on the floor — what happened to his pride? — and leans back against the couch, his head nestling in his lover's belly. There is an orchestra of digestion. Derek listens to the symphony of the food that he cooked being absorbed into his lover's belly. Against the back of his skull, he feels the muscles tighten and release with every breath. He closes his eyes, trying to ignore the dust he can see under the stereo cabinet, the cat hair woven into the rug. He is trying to capture this moment, to wrap this moment in something that he can remember. The warmth of his lover's belly, the sound of food passing through. Behind his eyelids, tears glimmer unshed.

His father would laugh to see him cry.

His father would laugh with a twist — cruelty.

His father.

Think of all the times he sat on the floor with his father, watching what appears to be the exact same game on the television, while his father, oblivious to his presence, cheered and groaned in chorus with the faceless crowd.

This morning, crying, Derek called his mother. He's having an affair, he said, his voice whiny and high-pitched to his own ears. He's going to leave. The stab of realization made him gasp, took his breath away.

(Don't cry. Crying is for girls and babies.

Weeping is for cocker spaniels.

Push it back. Swallow pain with one glass of water.)

His mother came over and stroked his forehead. Made him tea.

He watched expressions dance and shimmy across his mother's face. Worry. Relief. Hope.

Hope?

Could it be, that after all these years, his mother still has hope? Hope that he will move on, now that this man is disappearing, squirming from his grasp. Now, he will move on and find a nice girl to marry.

Can she be that naive?

Mother, he said to her, his voice cracking. Don't worry.

Just be careful, she said. Please. For me.

Be careful?

The lover half lifts off the couch. A cloud of cat hair rises and falls, settling on Derek's lap. Yes, the other man shouts, yes. Oh baby. Yes.

The puck flies into the goal again and again in instant replay.

Outside, the traffic hums by, and the wind begins to pick up. Tree branches sway and crack. The oak trees in the back yard fight mightily against the frigid forces.

The sound of one branch giving up, one branch breaking off, is like a human scream. Of course, they don't hear it over the shouts of the fans, the organ's harsh roar.

The howling gusts provide a backdrop for the silence as the man and his wife stare at each other across the dinner table. Between them a heaping plate of pasta steams, curls of garlic wafting in the air.

Going to be a cold winter, says the man, struggling to serve himself, the slippery noodles eluding his fork.

Will the trees be all right?

Oh sure, we may have a little damage. They'll stand up to worse. The guys should be around all week, keep an eye on things. Make sure the pipes don't freeze up.

Oh.

Listen to the knives and forks scraping against the everyday china. The man cuts his pasta. How gauche. The wife frowns and looks away. To spite him, she lights a cigarette before he has finished, allows the ash to fall lazily away onto her unfinished meal.

Don't need a ride in the morning, he gazes out the window. I'll take a cab.

Don't be silly.

What?

I always drive you to the airport. Always.

Not this time.

Yes. This time.

No.

Yes.

He sighs. Fine, all right.

The wife feels victorious, as though she has fought off invisible demons for one more day, and wonders why she cared so much. She hates to drive in the ice, particularly in the dark. And the drive to the airport is not a pleasant one at the best of times.

Look into her imagination:

the blue car slipping side to side on the dark highway.

Watch:

a meridian too close, another car skidding.

A bang that she can feel in her knees.

She blinks and draws deeply on the cigarette. Her heart patters unevenly, lightly. Best not to imagine, best to carry on.

She forces herself to stand, to clear the dishes off the table that the man made himself out of a fallen pine, the legs engraved with climbing roses always reaching towards the surface. Sometimes, as she sits at the table, and talks on the phone, her hand reaches down to the flowers. Her fingers trace over the detailed petals, the veined leaves. The pattern is becoming shiny and worn. Her touch is wearing it away.

Two plates, two glasses, two forks. She scrapes leftovers into the garbage. She can load the dishwasher in less than ten minutes. She has timed herself. In less than ten minutes.

Listen:

She can hear the man opening and shutting drawers in the bedroom. But what else? The unmistakable click of the telephone being lifted.

Walk away. She goes into the living room, where the man's voice will be too far away even to be a muffled suggestion, and turns on the stereo. Loud. Louder. She picks up her knitting, her fingers flying through the wool. Knit sweaters. Knit socks. Knit scarves. Knit hope.

She donates all her knitting to AIDS charities. The sacrifice is not enough. She would sacrifice more if she could. A knife blade, her own blood pouring out over an altar of stone. Her fingers have developed calluses, dry cracks on the tips that bleed in the cold. Picture the boys, all lined up in their sterile green beds, bulky scarves warming their throats, as though they are just about to leap up to go outside and play. Like children. Innocent children. As though all that is keeping them there is the bitter-cold winter day.

Did you get the ticket?

Yes.

And?

I can't go.
Can't? or won't?
I have work to do, deadlines. I have to ...
Yes?
Think, I have to think.
About what?
I don't know ... I just ...
What?
Work, I have work.
Bring it. You have to come. A whole week, imagine. Just us.
You mean, no wife.
No wife.
Why?
It will be fun. You'll see.
I don't know.
I need you. Please come.
I don't know.
Please.
OK.
Is this all we are ever going to talk about?

The girl packs her bag, her hands shaking slightly. A quiver. A moment that can be quelled with a quick shot of whisky. Dutch courage. She swallows away the thought of Harry and his letter, Harry trying to pull her back towards him. Harry. She swallows again, choking on the hot gold.

The twins are playing the violins like fiddles, and she taps her feet to the rising sound. Faster and faster.

Sometimes, one glass of Scotch gives her enough distance. She can view herself from far enough to be safe.

Tomorrow they will fly away.

The man, packing his bag, senses that he is escaping from himself and wants to congratulate himself on his own adventurousness. Of course, he has been unfaithful before, but never has he taken a woman on a trip, no woman except his wife. His wife, his wife. Always his wife. Now, another chance. He has no friends to tell, really, only friends they share, friends who would be shocked, disappointed.

Threatened.

Think of infidelity as less of a problem than alcoholism. He has a friend who drinks half a bottle of Glenlivet each night. Another friend has recently smoked himself to death — riddled with disease, he continued to puff away until the precious balance in his body between oxygen and carbon dioxide flipped the other way. Gone. He has a friend who goes fishing every weekend to avoid his wife and family, his son a junkie who breaks in to steal jewellery to hock for cash. Sometimes this friend just huddles into a tiny cabin, freezing, to get away.

Which of them is worse?

Certainly not this man, who is only seeking his own happiness.

Isn't that what it is all about? One day, you are here, the next, a tiny change, the straw that breaks the camel's back, and the next, you are gone.

He whistles as he fold shirts and pants into his worn leather bag.

The man thinks of the girl as a crystal, cutting through the mundane reality of his staid, dull life. He does not really think about his wife's feelings at all.

If the girl is capable of anything, it is forgetting. She prides herself on it. In her room, she folds a silk nightie and stuffs it into her canvas bag. She imagines how the man's eyes will light up when he sees it, feels his callused fingers pulling at it, imagines it sliding over her skin, smiles.

Harry's letter is forgotten in the festering waste of a dozen small sweater-clad dogs, dragged out for walks on the coldest days of December.

In the night the girl awakens several times. She is dreaming about sharks again, dreams she has not had since Harry left. She has not been in the water since, of course, and she would never have gone in the first place without his urging. His insistence. But still, in the night, sometimes she sinks beneath the green glass surface, past her own bubbles rising in slow motion to the surface. Sometimes, in the night, she turns around and around until she is dizzy and the green surface above her flattens and turns to glass and she rises but she cannot break through. She can look up and see the sun and sky and clouds, distorted but real. Distorted but unreachable. Sometimes she can look down and see the unmistakable shadow of white slide by, barely causing a current to flow past her legs, her torso.

She once saw an interview with a surfer who had been attacked by a great white shark. It was like, he said, being broadsided by a Volkswagen.

Sometimes in her dream she allows the shark to broadside her, allows it to bite. As if to say: So? And now what?

Sometimes it is a whole frenzy of sharks, writhing in ecstasy as she watches herself float among them, torn, ribbons of bright red blood undulating in the current like fine silk.

Always she awakens dripping with sweat, the blankets soaked, her heart racing.

And now what?

When she is awake she thinks only of the man.

This is true.

She thinks of him in ways she never thought of Harry. For example, she never used the word "love" before. Never. Not even loosely, in a sentence. And now the word seems to drip from her blood. Love.

And now what?

Harry's sharks still drift through her dreams.

Harry's letters still find her mailbox.

She asks him why he is so obsessed with sharks, why he can't stay out of the water. Why he always looks over his shoulder.

But they are beautiful, he gestures. He makes the sign for angels.

No, she says, they are eating, killing, prehistoric machines. Monsters. If they see you, she adds, they will kill you. You are a meal. You are food.

His eyes look away from her lips.

Food, she says again, enunciating clearly. You.

You don't understand, he spoke. You don't know. They never attack humans on purpose. Only by accident, mistaking them for something else.

The girl takes Harry's face and holds it in front of her, forcing him to watch her lips move. I think, she says (just to hurt him, of course). I think you only pretend to like them because really you are so afraid. Terrified. I think they scare the shit out of you.

What? He speaks the word in a rumbling, flat shout. An earthquake.

Too loud, she gestures.

What? He signs. Not afraid.

If you think you understand them, you can control them. I don't even think it is about sharks.

I think you try too hard to make everything mean something, he says simply.

Forget it, she says then.

Forget it.

Harry's face displays emotions as clearly as a child's. His lip is drawn in, his forehead pulled into a frown.

You don't know me, he says again.

She looks at him, his proud brown skin, straight nose, eyes black as ocean depths. Hair rippling down his back. The absolute stillness of his body.

Harry frightens her.

To make peace, she reaches out and begins braiding his hair. His eyes close. When the girl kisses him, she is aware of his saliva. Inside her, something shrinks away from his thick, heavy tongue.

Cringe.

It would be fine, if they didn't kiss at all.

His mouth covers hers like he is breathing through a regulator, sucking out all the air.

She gets up at dawn and cleans the apartment top to bottom with the harsh, eye-stinging cleansers that she normally doesn't use. Her hands are raw and red and smell of ammonia. She strips down to nothing and prepares the tub, climbing over the high edge, the freshly polished claws.

Soak in the tub filled with heady sweet rose oil. Soak until done, until forgotten.

The girl calls the cab to take her to the airport.

Last night's frigid gale has blown the sky clear of clouds, and now the day seems to hover, waiting, behind the canopy of haloed stars.

Looks like California is coming to you, the wife says, gazing with obvious pleasure at the clear black sky.

Doesn't get this cold in California.

No, I suppose not.

The air is so cold it prickles her lungs.

A cigarette, a lighter. The air is easier to breathe that way.

The man ignores his wife. He thinks about the girl, feels the heaviness of his own arousal.

The only indication that he knows his wife is there is that he is patting her leg as he drives, something he has not done for years. She stares down at his hand, suspiciously. It is kneading her leg, her white leg, now layered with cellulite. Squeezing. Rubbing. He does not seem to know he is doing it, but she will feel his hand there long after it is removed.

What is going on here? Unspoken words fill the silence. She lights another cigarette from the butt end of the last.

He leans across the front seat to peck her cheek as he simultaneously opens the door.

I wrote down the number by the phone in the kitchen.

Call me tonight?

Sure. Thanks for the ride.

The wife has the same feeling she used to get when she dropped her sons off at their friends' places for the weekend, drove them to summer camp. That she is the dull old woman, and they are vibrant, full of life, off to do and see things that she doesn't understand. She is losing him.

I love you, she says to the empty place where her husband sat.

Her hand holding the cigarette is trembling.

Stop. Open the windows, to let it escape. Let the cold air wash in and fill the car like water. Squint through the smoke into the mirror.

Be careful, the roads are glacial, laced with dark, hidden traps, camouflaged by the endless black and charcoal grey. Polished. The season is dark.

The wife merges into the slow stream of early morning traffic.

A cab pulls into the spot she has vacated. The woman does not see the girl emerging, the girl who first moves towards the man and then stops as he nods his head at the car. The girl is paralysed on the sidewalk, ice has crept into her veins and flash-frozen her into place. Her own cigarette drops from her fingers and rolls away. She is staring at the woman driving the blue car, staring with eyes like full moons, staring, in disbelief. Staring as though she could look into this woman's soul.

Leaving her bags on the sidewalk, near the man, the girl runs into the airport, runs down the tiled hallway, runs for the familiar picture of the stick woman with the triangle skirt, only barely making it to the stall before she is sick. Violently, unforgivably sick. The wife. Of course.

The first time she has seen the wife.

Was she really sick?

Or is it only the lurching of her own thoughts as she stands rooted to the sidewalk as the man gestures her to stay put at the same time as he waves his wife away.

Did she really run?

In her mind, a scene is written: the blue car, slipping on a glistening patch of unexpected ice. The woman driving the car is listening to the stereo symphony and hardly notices the car scuttling off the road. What's that? A truck, jackknifing on that same patch of ice. They are dancing around each other in a slow, uncertain circle. The body of the truck is tipping, the woman stares up as the music crescendos, watches the truck leaning towards her insignificant blue car, leaning. The woman does not hear the sound of her own car being crushed, does not see her own red blood coursing out of her body as rhythmic and sure as the beat of the radio that still tinnily plays a forgotten symphony.

The girl's face is blank, her jaw slack.

The accident plays out in her mind.

Are you all right?

What? Yes. All right.

What happened?

Nothing. It is just too early ... too early in the morning for me. Must have been sleeping with my eyes open.

She kisses the man breezily on the lips, tongue slipping into his mouth, aware of the glances of the other people in the line-up. The girl wears no makeup, her hair pulled back into a ponytail. She looks thirteen years old. Fourteen.

Do you think that's her father? A woman asks another, farther back in the line.

The little blue car flips and burns in the girl's mind, against the back of her closed eyelids. She grips his gloved hand more tightly in her own and tries to block out what she now knows: his wife has brown hair, worn short. His wife smokes. She drives a blue car. She listens to symphonies too loudly on her car stereo. She still takes her husband to the airport. Her coat is emerald green and hopeful.

File these facts away.

What has she done to this woman?

Killed her.

This man is her husband.

This will be so wonderful, the man whispers in her ear. Just wait.

She leans back against him, feeling his warmth through her jacket, feeling his solidity, his presence.

I saw your wife, she says. She ...

Shhhh.

No. She looks nice.

Ah. Well. She is ... nice. We won't talk about her.

No? What if I want to?

I don't.

What is her name?

Shhhhh.

The ticket counter:

Are you travelling together?

Why?

Are you travelling together? Do you have your ID?

Yes. Passports. (The girl's covered with coloured stamps, the man's all but bare, two blue marks).

How many bags?

No. Carry-ons. Two. That's all we brought.

Next please.

People swirl around the airport, thick parkas over summer dresses — the contrast is disturbing. They will go from cold to warm, winter to summer, in a few short hours. The girl sees the image of the woman, crushed and bleeding. Again and again, amidst the crowd of yawning, shivering people, she senses something slipping, something beginning, and she can't stop it now. She can't make it stop. I am going crazy, she wants to say. Craziness twists and turns in all the warm grey corners of her mind.

Take off your gloves.

Why?

I want to feel your skin.

The man takes her hand in his. His skin is smooth, yet feels thick and incorruptible, leathery. His thumb traces a pattern in her palm as they walk, and she lets herself be led towards the gate.

I saw your wife.

Is this all we are ever going to talk about?

The girl does not listen as the stewardess carefully instructs the correct way to fasten a seatbelt, does not pick up the safety brochure and pretend to examine it with great interest. She is looking out the window. The window itself is scratched and looks cracked, a tiny pinprick of a hole is apparent on the outer edge. She breathes deeply. Canned air. False air.

The ground peels away under the wheels and pressure sucks back in her head, causing her ears to pull and pop. Her ears pop just like they do when she is scuba diving, when she plunges so deep below the surface. But of course scuba diving makes her think of Harry, so she will not think of that now.

Are you afraid of sharks? She asks the man.

Sharks? On land or in the sea?

In the sea.

I don't swim.

Ah.

She is aware of the man holding her hand, looking over her shoulder out the window. Through the plastic, the landscape is grey and thick, although the sky is lustrous and blue. There is an illusion of warmth inside this impenetrable metal tube. Blue sky and sunshine. She sighs and sinks back into her seat.

He rings the bell for the attendant.

Could we get some blankets please?

Blankets?

Yes.

Do you need pillows as well, sir?

No, just the blankets.

The blanket is thin and small and barely covers their laps. Looking at him, she has an overwhelming desire to run her hands through his hair, to feel his scalp, the realness and nearness of him. She wants to put her nose in his ear and sniff, bite down on his shoulder. Taste blood.

He smiles, and wrinkles dance down from eyes to mouth. Tiny creases and crevasses she wants to taste with the tip of her tongue.

His hand sneaks over under the blanket and rests on her thigh. He thinks that if the plane crashes now he will not mind because he is with her. He has not given another thought to his wife, making her way home in the empty throbbing symphony of her car. His wife, who is right now thinking of what she will do to fill this lonely week, this void of hours.

The girl closes her eyes and leans back on his shoulder, allowing the wife and car and everything else to drop away under the tilting wing in the sun.

Behind closed lids, a scene:

Her own name being called over the loudspeaker at school. To the office. The principal's office. The jeers of her classmates: you're in trouble, big big trouble, you're in trouble. The long walk down the corridor, which smells of antiseptic and chalk dust. Chalk dust makes her sneeze. She arrives, eyes watering, counting her steps. Counting the lockers.

People in the office, waiting.

I'm so sorry, it's your parents, the principal is speaking, face looming over her like a bloated cartoon. Your parents. They ...

They're dead?

You knew?

You just told me.

You knew?

You just told me.

The girl's parents are dead, or mostly dead (but these details will be spared for later). She is fourteen years old.

Thank you, she says, and goes back to her classroom.

Thank you?

She used to believe in fairies. And angels.

Now, there is nothing left.

She turns to the man.

My parents didn't die in a plane crash.

Oh?

Remember Lockerbie?

Of course.

It happened on the same day. It seemed more ... glamorous. So I let people believe it.

So how did they die? A gentle voice, so kind.

Oh. They killed themselves. In a car. Carbon monoxide poisoning.

I'm sorry.

Me too.

The man traces circles on the inside of her thigh. Watches as her face fights her emotions.

Why? he whispers. He has to know, has to ask. Why?

The girl looks at him, hard in the eye. Her gaze is cold, ice tears frozen inside.

She had just found out that she had cancer, she couldn't face it. She thought she would go bald. Bald. So they decided to end it. So she wouldn't lose her hair. Her fucking hair.

That's awful.

Yes it is.

Poor baby.

No one even asked me what my parents were doing in Scotland.

No?

No.

The stewardess offers drinks.

Yes. Two. Scotch.

Are you trying to get me drunk?

Yes, so I can take advantage of you.

The man's breath is warm and alive in her ear, she can feel each pulse carrying his breath through her body.

Love, he is thinking. Love.

She falls into a warm drowsy sleep, devoid of dreams, as the plane wings through the sunlit skies.

I know you, she thinks she hears him whisper in her ear, his hand sliding deeper into the fold of her legs.

What were you dreaming about?

Nothing.

You were talking.

I was? What did I say?

Mumbling, really. I couldn't tell.

But I wasn't dreaming.

He fixes her with a knowing look.

I wasn't.

OK.

The girl sits and waits in the airport, freezing, despite the fact that it is a full thirty degrees warmer here than where they came from. Goose pimples rise up on her bare arms, she longs to put her winter coat back on but would feel too conspicuous amongst the bright colours of summer dresses that surround her. The winter here in California has been strange, as though God forgot to change the channel. Here it is still eighty degrees, here it is still summer. People seem to be happier, looser than back home in the cold. She sits up straighter and tries to will her body to absorb this heat, keep her from shivering, from seeming odd. Odd to be cold on such a hot day.

In the car, they argue over the radio station. He wants to listen to top 40 dance music, she prefers jazz, slow and rhythmic. At one point she says, act your age — you can't really like that stuff, it's for teenagers.

He thinks about his CD collection at home, the hundreds of albums he buys. He buys the steady beat of the drum and throb of the bass guitar. He can name any group and any song being played on the radio today. He has it piped in to the greenhouses.

The plants like it, he says, inanely, feeling ridiculous. Makes them grow.

She laughs, her hand resting easily in his crotch. He chooses not to argue.

They drive to the hotel listening to the tuneless jazz, each song blending into the next with no distinguishing stop and start.

The room is pale and beige and carpeted thickly and smells heavily of deodorizer and stale smoke. Is there a view? They don't look at anything but each other, anxiety is gone.

Watch:

The girl sinks to her knees and takes the man in her mouth.

In the mirror, he sees the image of the back of her head superimposed over his crotch, and explodes into her for ever.

She can't swallow fast enough, he drips from her chin. For the first time in her life, she does not rush to the bathroom to rinse her mouth. Instead, she curls into the crook of his arm and sleeps: in dreams she sees Harry in Japan, wandering around a store that sells only rice, searching the blank faces of the other shoppers, searching desperately for her. In her dream, the voice over the loudspeaker advertises a lost boy. In her dream, she and the man turn and walk from the store, bags of rice filling their shopping cart until it overflows.

I love you, the man whispers into her hair, when he knows she is asleep.

CHAPTER 4

Sunlight filters in through the open curtains. The warmth feels offensive, unclean.

The girl is alone. The man has gone to his conference. He is missing. Missing from the room. She feels the fierce possessiveness that a wife must. Like a wife, she muses, allowing the thought to coat her like dust before she shakes it off. No, she says out loud, not the wife. I am not anybody's wife.

The wife, at home, sings the familiar lyrics of a Broadway musical as she soaps her body in the shower. Her soapy hands lift her heavy breasts, lather the loose flesh of her stomach.

She touches her skin in places her husband's hands have never been. Never. Her skin is soft and pink, pink folding over purple. Soft. Her husband does not touch her with his hands any more.

Her husband — endless miles of trees and shrubs and still more trees visible from every window, behind her in every mirror.

Look:

His trees undulate under the cerulean dome of the winter sky, through the glass that she cleans every day. The glass sparkles in the heatless winter sun. The trees undulate.

Vinegar and newspaper are all you need to clean glass.

Rub it carefully and firmly, with vigour.

Do not leave any streaks.

In the spring and summer, the wife goes around the house and collects the corpses of the birds that fly into the glass and die from shock. Or massive head injuries. They never bleed. The bodies are weightless in her hand. She buries them in the garden, randomly, like flowers. Sometimes, when she is planting, she accidentally digs one up. Bones so fine they barely crunch against the blade of the shovel penetrating the dirt. Such tiny bones.

The girl spends the afternoon walking up and down the streets of the sleepy town, feeling the warmth of the sun on her long dark hair, occasionally reaching up and folding it into a ponytail, relishing the warmth against her hands. In her lungs, the heat feels heavy, like nausea.

She looks into the windows of stores but does not go in. The day is so bright that her own face is reflected back towards her, eyes the size of two moons in a tiny sky. Freckles that create a small galaxy over nose and cheeks.

Walk.

She paces up and down the street until she finds that her feet want to run, and, in spite of the fact that she is wearing summer sandals, she runs down the steep hilly street to the water and runs and runs until blisters form on her toes and her body aches with a satisfaction and finally, warmth, which she can shroud herself in.

It must look strange, the girl running. Her light cotton dress pressed close against her body, flowing out behind. Her sandals clattering on the hot pavement.

Silly to run in this heat.

Her legs stretch and sing, muscles pulling and pushing in perfect sync, rippling along her thighs and shins.

In the clothes she is wearing, the girl looks as though she is being chased.

Her heart thuds with thoughts of the man: she can't stop thinking of him, of his face and his hands and his voice. She hears herself speaking to him, suddenly nervous, maybe what she says is wrong, awkward, childish. Imagines that when she speaks her voice hits an awkward pitch — squeaks. She hears herself talking to him and feels panicky, she has said too much, she has said stupid things. He hates her. He must be laughing at her. She runs faster.

Muscles taut as violin strings pull pleasingly in her abdomen.

Keep running.

The man sits in his conference and listens politely to fertilizer salesmen and sprinkler experts, he listens to talk about new species of trees, bred to be hardier through the winter months, through droughts. He sees the girl, kneeling, her head pressed into his groin, and it is all he can do not to gasp out loud.

The girl, kneeling.

The girl finds herself running along a road that skirts the sea. There is no wide swathe of California sandy beach. Instead, jagged rock teeth rise from the surfy water. Seals and sea lions flop motionless on the outcroppings, so still they look like stone. Shiny wet stone. The girl slows down to look.

Behind her, a voice.

Her heart beat trips, startled.

What?

I said, they're a little messed up.

Who?

The pennipeds.

What?

The seals, sea lions. Usually they go a little farther south in the winter. El Niño I guess.

Oh, I guess. The girl catches her breath. Sure.

They stand silently and stare out into the grey-blue sea. Seals slip and slide into the water on their bellies, rolling through the waves.

Watch:

There is a furore in the water. Splashing.

The animals bark in an urgent key. Flop up onto the rocks. How can they climb up? No arms, no legs. Their bellies grab the teeth of stone. Fear is palpable. The air is rich with terror.

Damn, I missed it.

Missed what?

Shark attack, he says. The whites feed up here. It's a smorgasbord.

The water churns and churns and churns. Minute pass: five, ten, twenty.

The water churns.

For how long?

Finally, the water is still. Seaweed floats to the surface.

The seals lie on the warm rock, shiny, like pebbles in the sun.

The girl turns abruptly and starts half-walking, half-jogging back to the hotel. How can she not think of Harry?

Sharks and Harry go hand in hand.

Richard Gere is fifty, she says to the man at dinner.

So?

People wouldn't stare if he was with a younger woman.

The man laughs, and lifts his glass.

Robert Redford. Paul Newman. Even older.

I know, he says, more seriously. I'm not a movie star.

Doesn't matter.

I would hope not! He pretends to be offended.

All around the crowded restaurant, the girl feels the prickle of eyes on the back of her neck. Sparks. People staring.

What do they want?

Her hair burns angrily in the sun. The man goes to the washroom. She misses him when he is gone, left alone with all the eyes on her.

It's the nineties, she says to the man and woman at the next table. Get over it.

They ignore her, look past her out to sea.

Across the room, the man stares at the girl, alone. Watches as she lifts the glass to her full, moist lips. Watches as she sips the blood-red wine. She fingers a piece of bread, not eating it. She rolls the soft part into a ball and leaves it on her plate.

Her sunglasses hide her eyes.

The man has a pain in his chest that might be love. Or regret.

If he were only thirty years younger. Twenty.

No.

Shake the thought away. He whips his head back and forth like a dog, like someone with water trapped amongst the tiny bones and caves of the ear. Shakes his head.

If I were thirty years younger, he says, settling into his seat, the wicker biting into his spine.

Then what?

Then it could be for ever.

Do you think?

Yes.

Yes.

Picture the man in a younger form, hair unmarred by grey. Face unlined. Picture the girl standing next to him in church. White satin dress. Tuxedo.

Picture their children.

Picture an impossible life.

Touch:

He reaches over for her hand, cold in spite of the evening heat. Blue and green veins painted delicately on the inside of her wrist. Skin so painfully soft and smooth and tight. Skin that rises up in gooseflesh as he traces the pattern of vessels up towards her elbow.

They move closer together. People stare.

The girl glares over his shoulder at a doughy old man. He drops his gaze back into the bowl of soup that sits before him. Closes his mouth.

When the man touches her, her body lurches towards him, invisibly. The web around them pulls them together.

What do I see in him, she wonders, lovingly touching the bristles on the nape of his neck.

Lovingly.

His fingers move farther up her arm. Skin like velvet near the crest of her shoulder.

At the hotel, they make love ferociously on the tiny balcony of the room. The girl looks out towards the grey sea as he enters her from behind. Look up, she dares the people passing on the street below. Judge this.

She stares into the grey sea and sees white shadows looming just off shore. The man's heavy breath behind her makes her want to cry.

He fucks her harder.

Is this love?

He wakes up several times in the night and traces the knobs of her backbone with his fingers, winds his fingers around her rib cage. His body aches with desire, but also a more heady feeling — protective, strong. He wraps his thick arms around her, and she shifts in sleep, pressing her head deep into his shoulder, her nose pushing air across his throat. Her breath is hot and sweet.

Her eyes move behind closed lids.

Look inside her dreams:

The man swims on the surface, the green-glass surface. From below, she looks up, reaching. His body slices through the glass like a hot blade. Sun fills the space between them, perfect lines of light, distorted by the ripples he makes. Then, she is sinking.

The ocean floor pulls her down, brown kelp winds around her limbs.

She doesn't stop watching.

The white shark so far above, moving so quickly through the warm water. So much bigger than the man, moving so quickly.

White belly, grey scars.

Ribbons of crimson circling down through the water.

The girl wakes up, screaming. Her scream is soul-deep and loud. The hair on the back of the man's neck stands to attention. His heart beats in his throat.

What is it?

Eyes open, she blinks at him in the moonlight.

What is it?

Eyes closed, she sinks back into sleep without speaking. He is left awake in the strange room, the tiny girl (so fragile!) cradled in his arms.

What is he doing here?

The man buries his face in the girl's hair, inhaling the floral scent. Her legs entwine with his. An elbow pokes into his side.

The man is fifty-two. He feels nineteen.

Is that enough to equal love?

In the distance, the hum of traffic. A siren wails.

Listen:

Music pours heavily from the stage like a thick, syrupy sauce. Sweet and clear and vibrant. Let it pour over you, fill all the spaces.

The wife leans forward in her seat to see past the elaborate hairstyle of the woman in the next row. Derek, beside her, hums under his breath. His fingers drum the arm of the fake velvet chair. The music is playing in his mind, on a staff across his thoughts. His eyes search the orchestra pit, admiring the elegance of the black shirts and pants; his fingers play the melody on the arm of the chair. Pausing, his gaze settles on two blond heads bent over two violins. Identical. The boys are tall and slender, waving subtly to the beat of the song. In perfect sync. Derek closes his eyes. His head sways gracefully in the tide of sound. Twin violins. A composition forms unwittingly on the score behind his closed eyes.

A symphony writes itself.

The wife leans the other way, to try to peer through the gap on the other side. The hairstyle bobs and fills the space. She cannot see the stage, but she can hear the singer. A note is missed. She winces.

She once was a singer.

Is that true?

Imagine:

The wife as a young woman, voice lifting clear and sure into the back row of a crowded theatre. The quaver as her breath carries the high notes. The hushed appreciation of the crowd. Imagine the applause, the newspaper reviews, the admiration of family and friends.

Imagine the possibilities.

Of course, she got pregnant. She moved on.

That is what the wife does: she moves on. Singing? No more. Painting? No more. Knitting? Yes.

She could have brought her knitting bag to the theatre. She imagines it resting against her leg, the coarse wool snaking out over the smooth needles, emerging on the other side as a soft sleeve, or a collar. Rough yarn against her fingers.

She supposes Derek would have been embarrassed. The scent of his aftershave tickles her nose. She reaches out to pat his slender hand. Piano fingers, she murmurs.

Shhh.

Don't talk during the performance.

There is another scene that should be examined:

Halfway around the world.

A distance that can be covered in a breath. In a blink.

It is daytime in Japan, and Harry is walking through a garden of stilted plants, carefully pruned in immaculate shapes. Water drips and falls from miniature waterfalls that cascade into planters.

His walk is graceful, but heavy. His shoes slap against the paving stones.

Slap.

Drip.

Of course, he cannot hear it.

He is confused by all the precision. Irritated. He wants to see unruly plants leaping unchecked up the trunks of trees, flowers cascading in chaos through fields. The air is thin and sparse. His limbs feel awkward and heavy. He stumbles.

Drip.

He wants to go underwater and see the extravagant seaweed pulled back and forth by strong currents, stalked by viscous fish, eels. He is yearning to go under.

Water is heavier than air. Water keeps his body moving in a way he cannot accomplish on land. Underwater, time slides by softly. The silence is different, because it is intended. An intentional hush. Underwater, he can feel his own pulse so clearly, it feels like a sound.

Underwater, colours exist that cannot be imagined on dry land. Prismatic.

Colours within colours.

He is aware that he is alone.

The girl is gone.

He sees that in the row of paper lamps, swinging in the breeze. He sees it in the forced foliage. He smells it in the orchid-scented air.

He loved to leave her.

Inside the quiet caverns of his mind he envisions her with other men. He imagines her tumbling through white sheets, awash with sweat, climbing on men's bodies. Brown-black freckles sprinkled on her white hot back. Rage.

Truth is variant:

he loved the way they looked together. Dark and pale. Tall and short.

he loved her because she never once mentioned his deafness.

he hated her because she never once mentioned his deafness.

Do you want to hear the story?

No. Not yet.

Harry won't tell his story. Wrap it up tightly under the thick brown paper of silence.

The water drips precisely into a series of pools built into the rock garden.

Drip.

Stars glisten like beads of sweat across the sky.

When's Dad coming back?

Oh, Friday. Late. Why?

Just wondered, d'you think he'd be interested in ...

In what?

Never mind. Nothing.

Oh.

Mom?

Yes?

I ...

Are you OK, Derek?

Of course, I just ...

What is it?

Nothing, Mom. Love you.

He turns away and leaves her at the door of her small blue car. It looks like a toy. It makes her look large, too large to fit behind the toy-sized wheel, through the toy-sized door. She looks at her watch, it's late, she would have missed her husband's call. If he bothered. The night air is heavy and hostile.

The air makes her lonely.

She is a giant, crammed into her tiny car. She drives towards home and stops at a coffee shop that is full of young people. Small, lithe. She feels them looking at her as she sits down alone and pretends to read the paper. What am I doing here, she thinks, what am I doing?

She forces herself to stay and drink the whole cup of coffee, slowly. Three cigarettes, one after the other. A grey haze mask.

Observe the people in the room:

The girls dressed like hippies wearing two-hundred-dollar shoes, the boys posturing, all of them pretending. The wife pretends to belong, pretends that this is not so unlike her that it makes her nervous. A sweat dampens her palms.

Is it hot in the room? Cigarettes, heating the air. Rivulets of sweat run down her forehead. The change of life? Is that what it is, menopause? Or is it something more sinister, something more like fear?

At home, she makes herself some hot chocolate and takes it to bed with her. The emptiness of the bed is a pleasure, yards of cool cotton uninterrupted in their smoothness. No body heat or stale breath to move away from. No snoring to break the stillness.

There is too much glass in the house. The glass is clean and haunting. The stars shine through the skylights.

The glass is cruel and taunting.

Now I lay me down to sleep, she whispers, I pray the Lord my soul to keep. If I should die before I wake, I pray the Lord my soul to take. Our Father, who art in Heaven ...

She has no idea why she is praying.

Alone in the hotel again, the girl awakens feeling irritable and tired.

Her period? No.

This is a different kind of fatigue. A deeper, harder languor. The walls of this tiny room sink towards her. Breathe deeply. The air is laced with the chemical cold of air conditioning. Cool, but metallic.

She lies on the bed and carefully measures the weight of the stories he has told her: of meeting his wife, of his children growing up, his daughter's wedding, his first dog, the time he went sailing on English Bay and capsized. Are they personal enough? Is he giving her enough? He told her of his first girlfriend, the way he broke her heart when he met his wife. He told her of the first time he had an affair. It was just sex, he said. Not like this.

Really?

Not like this?

She doesn't give anything back. Not Harry, not anything. She imagines herself saying it:

I was married myself, once.

When I was twenty-one.

We lasted three weeks. We lasted for ever. Then he hit me.

A purple-blue bruise seeping into the skin around my eye, staining forever and forever.

She doesn't give this to the man. She makes things up.

Liar.

Her hands feel for the valleys near her hip bones, the cage around her heart. She feels bloated and unsteady and after she has thought enough, enough already, she sinks back into sleep, a long-lost friend. She sleeps until noon in the flickering light of the television. Free porn in this hotel. Imagine. She half-wakens, watching pneumatic breasts and stilted dialogue. Imagines the man watching the same film, masturbating. Would he be aroused? She squints suspiciously at the grunting, sighing women.

Her own body is bony and sharp and her breasts are tiny. She is wasted and ugly, her stomach an indecent protrusion within her heap of bones.

Change the channels. Voices rising and falling. Talk shows.

Turn it off.

She leaves the hotel room, unshowered, wearing running shoes and shorts with one of the man's undershirts. Today she will really run.

Freedom drifts on the California breeze. El Niño. This year, there are no seasons, only earthquakes to punctuate seasons like the end of sentences. The autumn broken by the big quake, delineating that moment from winter. The sidewalk is rippled with seismic scars, bucking gently under foot like waves.

The locals wear sweaters, in spite of the heat, waiting for the chill they know will be coming, that has always come.

Damn weather, they curse in the streets. Goddamn, El Niño. Don't know if we're coming or going.

Others relish the unexpected Indian summer, sit in their gardens looking puzzled, yet pleased. As if they don't know who to thank. As if they don't know what will happen next.

She runs through the downtown, past the university where the man listens, takes notes, and collects brochures and magazines. The buildings are large and ominous with huge windows, a million eyes. Her feet thud the pavement. Familiar. Breathe in and out. Feel the heart accelerate to accommodate the demands of the muscles. In and out. The air smells pulpy and of grass going to seed. California. Her eyes do not focus on anything except the piston action of her legs, she can feel the pulse in her wrists, on her neck. The air is rough and burns her throat. Her lungs drink hungrily from the heat.

The man touches her so gently, as though she might break.

She might break. She is fragile, like a tiny bird.

She is strong, like iron.

She runs the syllables of the man's name into the pavement with her flying shoes. She runs the image of his face into her heart. She runs until Harry is blurred and unsteady, until she cannot remember what he looked like when he walked away.

Why do people who jog always look like they are grimacing? She hears someone ask.

Because they are in pain.

Voices not attached to faces. She runs into her hallucinations.

For how many hours can she run? How long?

Heat shimmers above the cracked blacktop.

Run towards the water, but don't stop and look at the seals languishing on the rocks. Don't stop and look at any disturbance in their midst. Sharks circle endlessly through the rocky islands. Don't look. Instead, focus on the clouds gathering on the horizon. Thick and black, threatening. Heavy with moisture.

Run.

It is hot. Steam rises from her shoulders, a fine layer of sweat making her skin glisten.

She runs until the light begins to dim, then, turning to go back up the hill, she trips.

Sidewalk and cement press against her cheek. She is aware of its heat and wonders if her face is burning. A fire. Her breathing is shallow. The sound of falling had been a snap. A snap? Perhaps a break. It takes several moments for her to pinpoint the source of the pain, the grey circles of shock gathering in a tiny flock before her eyes.

Someone helps her into a taxi.

Someone pays the driver to take her to the hospital.

Bodiless hands direct her this way and that.

The weather is beginning to change.

Rain flicks Harry's face like bacon grease. Sizzling. It mixes with the salt spray that clings to his skin. The boat rocks back and forth.

Wait for the signal. Now. Drop backwards into the water. The first moment is like orgasm, disorienting and freeing. Pull the clean oxygen into hungry lungs.

Sink down into the blue-green depths.

Falling, he relishes the pressure of the water. Watches the other divers drifting down around him. Perfect.

His hair swirls around unchecked. He imagines this is a disguise.

Mako have been spotted in the vicinity. Someone last night mentioned a hammer-head. Not a white. But still ...

His eyes scan the depths.

In the boat, the men are talking, talking about Harry, of course.

I don't think he can hear, one says to the other.

Of course he can, he just doesn't speak Japanese.

No, says the other, I'm pretty sure.

Deaf as a log.

The men laugh.

Tonto, they say. Hi Ho Tonto.

One of the boys speaks English. Don't, he says.

If you don't speak the language, such a short word can sound like a grunt, a noise disappearing into the wind and sea.

The men stare down into the murky water and watch the trail of Harry's bubbles.

Nice day, says one.

Every day's a nice day to you.

Ah, be quiet.

The boat rocks gently in the waves.

Below the surface, dim light filters through and illuminates the shallow water. The ocean floor is covered with long green weeds with bubble-crusted stalks. A grassy alpine meadow, submerged. A field of alien green wheat. Colourful fish dart in and out. Harry holds as still as he can, squinting as hard as he can. The other men collect scallops. He looks for the grey and white shadows. He looks for the triangular fins. Teeth. He hangs upside down in the water, to demonstrate his skills. He is motionless. The current has no power.

A turtle swims by, staring at him suspiciously, almost angrily, before disappearing behind the reef.

The girl blacks out in the taxi and has a hard time struggling to the surface again. The driver of the cab stands over her, slapping her face and yelling something that she takes to be a Russian obscenity.

I'm all right, she says. Jesus. Leave me alone.

She hops into the Emergency, trying not to look too ridiculous. While she waits, she picks the gravel out of her cheek, hoping it isn't as bad as it feels.

Can you come and get me?

Where are you? God. Where the hell are you?

I am at the hospital.

Hospital? Are you hurt? What happened?

I am at the hospital, can you come and get me?

I am on my way.

The girl maxes out her credit card paying for the elastic bandage and crutches. The doctor thinks maybe her ligaments have been torn, but, understanding that she has no money, agrees that ice and elevation will do the trick until she can go home.

Heart in his throat, the man speeds through the unfamiliar streets to rescue the girl.

He went for lunch today, well, beer really, with some other men. One had recently married a woman twenty years his junior. Lolita, one of them had joked. He should be arrested for pedophilia. Lolita. Twenty years. That would make the woman somewhere in her thirties. The man thinks: if he is a pedophile, what does that make me? Sick. He tries to laugh. Sick, but lucky. The girl is twenty-three.

Dear God.

He is in California, speeding towards the hospital.

The clouds open, and the rain begins to fall.

She can't walk, and is clumsy on the crutches. Seeing her, he is at once relieved and concerned. Only her ankle — still she cannot walk. He knows how important it is to her to run. He knows. He holds her while she cries, briefly, on his shoulder. A cry that turns into a laugh, bordering on hysterical. I guess I shouldn't have come, she says, wobbling on her crutches like a newborn heron. Your fault! She points a crutch at him.

Sorry, he says. But he sounds so helpless and forlorn that she laughs again.

Silly, she whispers.

At the hotel, they make love, her leg propped high on the pillow while he enters her again and again, his pale little tear-stained Lolita.

Did you ever see that movie Lolita?

No, but I read the book.

It was a book?

Of course.

Feeling stupid, the man stops talking. A book.

That evening they drive and drive and drive. He wants to show her the redwood forest, the magnificent wonder of ancient trees. They drive through one tree that is twenty-five feet around. A sign, posted to the side, brags that this redwood is estimated to be two thousand four hundred years old.

The trees shelter them from the rain.

Is that possible, asks the girl. Two thousand four hundred years?

The man is in awe of these woods. The girl is made to feel claustrophobic. Ankle throbbing black and blue under the expensive bandage. She only cheers up when she sees the junk haulers pulling discarded cars out of the rest stops. Her hand warm in his lap, she laughs.

The man begins talking.

Voice rises and falls as his past breathes.

Wait.

Listen:

Brought my kids down here once, in the camper. All three of them. All that noise — are we there yet? I have to go to the bathroom. When are we going to eat. What are we going to do next. Derek's got the window seat. Jamie keeps pushing. Mom. Dad. On and on. But it was great.

A camper?

Yes, a camper. The kids had a great time, we camped under the trees. I took them fishing in the river. I taught them all to fish. Tie flies. Cast the hook.

Fishing?

Yes.

Even the girl?

Yes, of course. It was Thanksgiving in Canada. My wife barbecued a turkey.

Your wife?

Yes.

Isn't that a man's job? The barbecue?

Huh?

Never mind.

She wants to slap him. Force him to look at her.

Is this all we are ever going to talk about?

I miss my kids, he says, simply.

They're still around.

Yes. But not kids. Not interested in going camping with their old man.

Yeah. Well. Maybe they'll have kids one day, you'll be a grandpa.

Oh.

Don't you think?

But I am already.

What? Already what?

A grandpa. Three grandchildren. I thought you knew.

No.

The dynamic changes between them, subtly. A kaleidoscope out of balance.

The wife is talking on the phone to her other son, Steven, the one who lives too far away to visit, the one with three children of his own, two boys, one girl. The distant son. His voice is bathed in static. He lives in the north — so far north — felling trees for a huge salary. Felling the trees that his father grows.

No.

Felling wild trees, unfarmed. Far out in the wilderness.

If a tree falls in the forest, does it make a sound?

Families are strange, cruel groups of people. Each generation knocking down the one before, leaving only roots and stumps.

How are my little angels?

Great, Ma. Really good. How are you?

Me?

Yeah, you. How are you? Dad still a miserable old bastard?

I'm fine. Don't speak about your father that way. He's very ... well. He seems happy.

Happy? Dad? Is he having another affair?

What kind of question is that?

Just kiddin', Ma. How are the Christmas trees, Dad really plant them?

Yes, you saw them. In the summer.

I know, I just thought he might have changed his mind.

You are coming down to help?

Of course, wouldn't miss it.

Good. That'll be good. (Another affair?)

I have to go, Ma. Kids want to go play outside. Teachin' them how to hunt like an injun.

Honestly, Steven.

What?

Never mind.

Bye Ma.

Bye sweetie, kiss my angels for me.

Sure.

Another affair?

Wood is stacked uselessly beside the fire. The wife kneels in front on the cold, hard slate. Another affair?

She stuffs in some paper. Shakes a spider out of the wood and lets it escape into the carpet. Arranges the wood carefully, boy scout style. The boys just finished scouts a moment ago. Years ago. A lifetime. For a second, she allows herself to be afraid. It's all slipping away. Where did it all go? One life. Hers.

The matches keep blowing out before the fire will light. Wind whispers down the chimney, into her bones.

Give up.

She curls up in the chair that the man has claimed as his, curls up in the scent of him and flicks on the television, jumping from channel to channel to channel.

Is he having another affair?

Does the son know of others?

Does she?

The girl and the man stop for dinner at a tiny diner hidden at the base of a tree in the woods.

Like Winnie the Pooh!

What?

All the houses in the trees. It's like Winnie the Pooh.

Right. Piglet's house, he says, and opens the door for her to follow.

They eat and drink — thick, juicy burgers and heavy homemade fries, lemonade made from real lemons and a mountain of sugar, and blackberry crisp coated with nuts and spice and oatmeal. The girl can barely swing on her crutches back to the car, she is so full. Waistband digging into her tiny belly.

We'll have to think of some way to work this off, she says.

Yes.

Any ideas?

Yes.

They park at a deserted rest stop in the shadow of the giant trees, and make love roughly in the car. Her ankle bangs against the back of the seat and she tries not to cry out in pain. He takes a long time. Over his shoulder she can see through the ceiling of branches to the stars so far ahead, peeking through the clouds.

Star light star bright first star I see tonight I wish I may I wish I might have the wish I wish tonight.

What to wish for? For the intervening thirty years to disappear? The wife to disappear? She shifts her weight so her head does not bang against the armrest, slides her hands around him and whispers into his ear until he shouts and falls down onto her, crushing her. The pain feels good. The pain cleanses her.

Getting too old for this, he sighs, lifting himself off her.

Never, she laughs. Never too old.

Hobbling back around the car to the front seat, she feels him dripping from her own numbed core. Never too old.

Walking through the hotel lobby, they stop to purchase two giant cups of coffee at the café. The shabby lobby belies the comfort of the rooms. An old bedraggled woman scuttles past.

Sinner, she hisses at the girl.

What? Pardon?

Sinner! The voice is a scream, a howl. People turn to look, to stare.

What?

A bellman hurries towards them, grabs the woman by the elbow. Mrs. Godwin! He yells. You can't shout at people!

You're shouting at me!

So you can hear me!

They disappear out the swinging door, swallowed by the night. The coffee cup shakes in the girl's hand.

Can you at least hold this? she snaps at the man. It's a little hard to carry when you're crippled.

Oh. Yes.

They are silent in the elevator, watching numbers flash by, ignoring their own reflections in the mirrored walls.

Sinner.

Back in the room, the man picks up the phone. Sorry, he says. I have to do this. Why don't you go out onto the balcony?

Why?

I have to make a call.

So?

Please go outside.

The wife, always the wife.

Sinner.

The girl shivers on the balcony, her foot dangling over the edge, the road twenty stories below. Just a tiny movement and she would be over. Would he be sorry?

Suicide is a sin.

Under her breath she chants the old familiar words, so well rehearsed in boarding school: Our Father who art in Heaven, hallowed be thy name.

She can't hear the conversation.

... thy kingdom come thy will be done on earth as it is in heaven.

Hi.

Hi honey, how's your conference?

Good. It's good. Raining here, not too cold.

Lucky you. I think it's going to snow.

A pause. Then — I saw Derek last night.

That's ... nice.

And I spoke to Steven, he'll be down soon.

Great! That's good. He can help out.

Are you having an affair?

What?

I'm asking.

What?

Tell me.

I don't know what you are talking about. Have you been drinking?

No.

I'm not having an *affair*. Don't be ridiculous.

Am I being ridiculous?

I'm much too old for that.

Is that the only reason?

What? Why are we talking about this?

How's California?

It's good. It's raining, I told you. But it's good to go outside with no jacket.

I'll pick you up tomorrow then. Nine o'clock?

Nine o'clock.

I love you.

Bye.

How's the little woman? The girl has hopped back into the room, letting bitterness coat her words.

Don't talk about her.

Excuse me?

Don't talk about my wife.

I don't ...

No matter how I feel about you, she will always be the mother of my children, my grandchildren.

Your wife is the mother of your grandchildren?

Don't be obtuse.

Obtuse? Big word.

The mother of my children, grandmother of my grandchildren.

I see. The matriarch.

Drink?

Yes.

Stuff the anger under the mattress, like so much unwanted dust. It is so easy to fall back into this embrace, to want nothing but to feel skin under fingertips, kiss gently the pink folds of an ear.

It is enough, for now.

The man gently places ice and cold cloths over the girl's black-and-blue ankle, her swollen and distended foot.

My poor baby, he murmurs. Poor angel.

It'll be fine.

Does it hurt?

Not too much.

The week is almost over. Another lifetime.

Harry is thinking about going home.

He sits in the bar with some American students, talking about the dive. Rather they are talking, and he is carefully watching their mouths.

You don't say much, do you?

He shakes his head and says flatly — no, I'm the strong silent type.

They all stop talking and stare at him. Too loud, probably. It is always so hard to tell how much force to put into his words, how much air to blow into them, in a place as crowded and probably noisy as this.

It's all right, he says, modulating his voice more carefully.

Underneath the table, his hands spell out the words, a habit he has been trying to break. He is relieved when they start to talk again.

The eels were amazing, says one.

I've seen bigger, another brags, in Australia. Twice the size.

Harry leans forward so he can watch more closely. Eels. This is what he understands. When he can, he breaks into the conversation.

I study sharks, he says carefully. Who here has seen a white?

All of them. Everyone has. They all have a story.
He settles back to watch them talk.

CHAPTER 5

Some days have no boundaries, blurry amorphous edges of morning into night. Some are tightly confined by barbed-wire time, restricting and sharp.

The looming flight will take them back to reality, away from themselves.

What can be done?

The girl and the man move through the streets silently, slowly. The girl begins to develop blisters under her arms from the crutches. Passersby keep stopping to give advice. They're too long for you, dear. Try making them shorter, or taller. Move the handholds higher, or lower. Everyone has a story. I was on crutches for six months, I was on crutches for three years. They laugh and smile and are polite, and the girl watches the man out of the corner of her eye, watches him listening.

Each time, he adjusts the crutches according to the advice. Her armpits seethe.

He drags her into an alcove outside a closed shop and kisses her so hard he draws blood on her lip.

Watch.

They look like they are starring in a movie with no plot, just an endless sequence of kissing and touching and gazing.

Skin grazing skin can form lasting scars.

She memorizes the way his skin folds under behind his ear when he turns his head. He stares at the way her hair springs free of its elastic and blows around her face.

The wife goes out early in the morning, drives around and around on the icy roads. Is he having another affair? Another affair?

When was the first?

Stop.

The cemetery floats by the window. White on grey on charcoal on black. No colours. She stops the car. The grass has turned a dull green, patches of bare dirt revealed like the scalp of a balding man. The headstones crumble and dissolve. Under her feet, the bones are crunching.

On her mother's grave, she places a poinsettia, purchased at a grocery store. Petals red and green are impossibly vivid through the grey. The pot is weightless. Can't stand upright in the winter wind, scattering across the hard grey ground. The pot cracks. The wife, unable to stop herself, pictures her mother lying in the bottle-green velvet-lined casket, eyes and lips sewn shut, pictures her mother lying there under the six feet of grey clay, although she has been down there for enough years that she is not lying there at all. Grey dust. Her mother would disapprove of the mess she has made, would frown at the scattering flowers. A red petal from a poinsettia drifts by at eye level, lifting higher and higher towards the flat grey sky. She sighs, sits on the cold grey stone. Her fingers scratch at the ground, so cold, like ice; so ungiving, like death.

Sometimes she wants to crawl down, farther and farther, tunnel through the unyielding earth and curl up in the crook of her mother's arm and let sleep take her away, anywhere else but here.

Sometimes.

Driving back home, she does not turn the radio on. Instead, she hums to herself, hearing the music vibrate in the back of her throat. Hymns. She hums the ancient hymns that she only vaguely remembers the words for, hymns she learned a lifetime ago at Catholic school, kneeling on the floor of a shiny gymnasium, her voice lost amongst the dozens of identical little girls stuffed into itchy wool socks and jumpers.

Onward Christian soldiers, marching as to war, with the cross of Jesus, going on before.

The cemetery drops into the background, a swathe of grey in the rearview mirror. It is Christmas, after all. There is colour in the town.

Department stores glide by her car windows. Stores decked out with boughs of oversized holly. Flashing, demanding Christmas lights. Music is piped into the street, and she must sing more loudly to drown it out.

Adeste fidelis, joyful and triumphant, o come ye o come ye to Bethlehem. Good King Wenceslas looked out, on the feast of Stephen.

Traffic moves at a crawl, the roads are glossy and slick, sprinkled with confection sugar. Sprinkled with sand and salt.

Nothing is real.

Her hands on the steering wheel are turning white. She has forgotten to turn on the heat. Her breaths hang in front of her like little clouds, the windows steaming up with her carbon dioxide, her exhalations. Through the haze, the lights look almost pretty, the holly looks almost real. She drives into a crowded parking lot, edging her tiny car into an impossible spot.

Blue paint scrapes off against the lamppost with an angry shriek.

Why doesn't she notice?

Buy something. Buy more. She stands in line-ups, purchases stacked in front of her. She can't stop buying.

It makes her light-headed.

By the time she gets home, she feels hot, almost feverish. Her purchases spill out onto the bed from the dozens of awkwardly sized plastic bags, expensive paper bags with rope handles.

What has she bought?

Promises:

Face cream and eye colour and hair dye and clothes, lingerie, nail polish. Her husband is coming home tonight. She wants to surprise him.

The girl and the man surprise each other.

The girl crutching along beside the man, feels her arms begin to weaken from bearing her weight. She is so tired that sometimes the ground seems to tip and she wobbles, sways from side to side. They cannot go back to the hotel because they have already checked out. The time is swirling by, like water down a bathtub drain.

What will happen next?

They both are looking into the uncertain future and demanding an answer. The sign in the bookstore window beckons them, was made for them.

Futures Read Here.

The girl spends an hour of their precious time browsing through the books, hesitant to go behind the dusty curtain into the back of the shop. Futures Read Here. She buys a first edition Faulkner for fifty cents as well as a pile of others to disguise her find: a fifties encyclopedia of everything, a Sears catalogue from 1942, a book of Ansel Adams photographs. Her purchase comes to forty-two dollars and twelve cents, and she can hardly keep from gloating.

The girl wastes an hour of their precious time.

Breathe.

The air is dusty and full of mould spores and history.

The man and the girl duck behind the velvet curtain and allow themselves to be pointed into the worn brocade chairs, part with more money, hold their hands out like paupers begging for change. Skin. An offering.

In the man's hand, the fortune teller (who, strangely, is a teenage boy with a wild array of sherbet colours in his hair) says he sees money. You work hard, he says, his voice a singsong. You make a lotta money. You have conflict. You are loved by many. But you make conflict. You like a little boy in a man-suit.

His laugh is high-pitched and curls through the lavender-scented air. You a strange man, like little boy. You don't know from love. But you, maybe you make a lotta money.

The man snatches his hand back as though burned, but smiles in his good-natured way. I see. Must be my inner youth.

The air smells of burnt flesh.

Inner youth, the ice-cream-haired boy laughs. Inner youth.

He reaches for the girl's hand and turns it over, his fingertips caressing the inside of her wrist.

Touch.

The hairs on her arm rise in protest.

His fingers are impossibly cold.

Strange that he speaks English as though it is a second language, this pallid white teenager who looks as though a skateboard should be attached permanently to his feet.

You an artist, maybe, he says, slowly. That's all. You alone. You make words, in your head maybe. That is all you ever have, just words. You not real, maybe.

The last statement is loud and not melodic, as though he has come up for air after being under water.

I don't see nothing else, he says. Nothing. Go home.

He laughs, maybe you a ghost! Boo! Spooky!

They all smile and thank each other politely, the girl, the man, and the seer. Thank you. Thank you. Thanks. Have a nice day.

The sun feels strange on their skin when they step out the door; the man loaded down by books is unable to support the girl who tilts on her crutches like a marionette with a broken string.

Why do I feel like I've been taken for twenty bucks?

Taken?

The kid was full of crap, you know that.

I don't know, I thought he was ...

What?

Creative.

Yeah, well. He's the one who is going to be making a lot of money. The man squints up at the white orb of the sun. It's getting late, we should start to head out.

Steam rises off the sidewalk where the sun heats yesterday's rain.

They arrive at the airport two hours early, sit and drink coffee and eat chocolate doughnuts and watch the planes rise and fall, lift dreamily heavenward through the shimmer of the hot blacktop, and float back to earth with tiny bounces and wobbles, get used to the ground once more. The girl and the man hold hands.

Watch:

Her tiny hand resting gently in his.

His thumb traces the bones on the back of her hand. Her knuckles.

Her hand is limp, in his.

Her ankle throbs, the veins in her foot pulse with a dark, black ache. The sweet doughnut sits in her stomach, roiling, as though her body does not quite know where to place it. And still, as she stares at the web of lines around the man's eyes, half listens to his voice speaking about learning to fly in a crop-duster on his friend's farm when he was twelve, she is happier and more at home than she has ever been before.

There is a warmth around her heart; it is carried throughout her body on a network of veins.

The man is caught up in his own story:

The wheat, from any height at all, looked like water, flowing through fields, do you know? It was all I could do to keep the nose of the plane up, when all my instincts told him to point it down, to dive it into the ground, into the yellow pool of wheat. Like being afraid of heights not because of the possibility of falling, but rather the possibility of jumping.

A pause.

How he could almost see the ripples that would flow outward in circles from the place where his plane would break the surface and dive down farther and farther into the earth. How he knew he would never be a pilot, that he belonged on the ground.

Love.

Of course, the girl says, looking deep into his hazel-green eyes.

You belong with your trees.

That's right, he breathes, with deep contentment.

But I belong with you, her eyes say into his, and he keeps her quiet with a kiss, his mind already in the little blue car, rushing away from the airport and this city of sun towards the icy cold acreage where his trees, sentries, stand in wait.

Do you love me? he asks, an afterthought.

What?

Do. You. Love. Me.

What a question.

Do you?

You're married.

Yes. But I think ...

Let's not say it.

Is this all we are ever going to talk about?

A plane did crash in Lockerbie, Scotland, on the day the girl's parents chose to die. Think about that. What were the passengers doing when the flying vessel began to drop? Had the stewardess begun serving the drinks? Perhaps their hands were reaching for more Clamato juice, another can of cola, when the lurch caused the drink cart to hit the ceiling.

A pocket of air, they might have thought. A fall, controlled, that has an end.

There is no end.

Did the flight crew die instantly, the sharp descent causing them to smash on the ceiling alongside the peanuts and beer? While the others, still confined by their seatbelts, watched, helpless, feeling their ground, their gravity, pulling them towards the rooftops?

And what of those on the ground — did they have time to look up, see the silver metal perhaps on fire, perhaps smouldering, pouring down on them like a sudden summer rain?

Rain made of shiny metal blades and fire.

How long did it take?

The girl shudders and presses her head back into the orange seat. She holds the man's hand firmly in her own. Out the window, the ground has disappeared beneath the cotton puffs of cloud. The man appears to be asleep, a half-smile plays at the corner of his mouth.

If the plane crashed, right now, they would land in the thousand-year-old forest. The trees would slice into the plane like a surgeon's scalpel. They would be torn apart.

Excuse me miss, the stewardess says, would your father like a drink?

My father is dead, the girl says back, deadpan. But I am sure my lover would enjoy a nice glass of Scotch.

Oh, she says. Of course.

The man laughs, and kisses the girl sleepily on the cheek, and she buries her nose into the concave bend below his collarbone, breathes in so sharply that she becomes dizzy.

She cannot inhale enough of him to keep him.

Breathe in. Breathe in. Breathe in again.

It is never enough.

Excuse me, the man says to the back of the stewardess, could we get a blanket here?

The plane lands smoothly, skating in on the runway like a Zamboni.

A yellow cab carries the girl back to her apartment, back to Faithful Street. Boys and girls come out to play, she whispers, and join your playfellows in the street.

It isn't until she turns the key in the lock that she realizes that once again she is terribly, terminally alone, and her arms and shoulders and legs ache from the effort of carrying, up the stairs, her bag and her books, hooked under her fingers. It is only seven o'clock, but still, fully dressed, she sinks into her bed under layers of fluffy white feathers and falls sound asleep, aware of the ringing phone and the sound of her own voice echoing around the rooms, but unable to reach up through the dense fog of sleep to catch it. Unable to surface.

It is seven o'clock and the moon is a sliver, masked with cloud, a capital C in reverse, dangling. Sharp.

The man has managed to keep his wife from speaking all the way home from the airport by turning up the volume on the radio and listening hard, with intent, as though receiving some kind of benediction from the Pope. She never interrupts when he is listening to the news. Her hair is newly red, conditioned and soft, hanging to her chin. Her hands on the wheel are decorated with deep blood-red polish. Underneath her sleek, new, black wool sweater and tights she is wearing more lace than has touched her skin in years, and a cloud of floral scent blankets her with sensuality.

An armour of femininity.

Say nothing.

Let the silence speak for itself.

The man wants to hold — for one more hour — the image of the girl, foot up on mounds of pillows, opening herself with her hand and welcoming him in. The smell of her sweat after her run. The sound of her voice. The delicate, bruised, tiny bones of her ruined ankle.

I thought we could go out for dinner, the wife is saying. I have a surprise.

What?

Out for dinner, a surprise, she says patiently, as though she is speaking to an old person who is more than slightly hard of hearing.

OK. That would be fine. He pats her leg. Did you do something to your hair?

Yes.

Oh.

Do you like it?

Sure. It's fine.

Music to my ears, dear.

What do you want me to say?

Nothing.

In the restaurant he is moody and aloof, noisily demanding bread from a passing busboy.

What's wrong?

Nothing. Must be tired.

Long day?

Yes.

She waits until the steaks are on the table, glistening with marble waves of fat and sauce. Waits until the potatoes have been sliced open and filled with butter to melt.

Despite himself, the man begins to relax. The food is delicious.

The girl, back at her apartment, is trapped in the cottony whiteness of sleep without dreams.

The man begins to notice that his wife is not that old, at all. That her eyes sparkle in the candlelight, that her hands are still small and soft.

She's having a baby, she says.

Who is?

Jamie.

My little girl, he thinks. A baby. The meat slides down his throat, a lump of gristle.

His little girl is pregnant.

His baby.

The earth spins faster, adding years to his life. The meat glistens with fat and slides on the china plate in a puddle of grease.

Life is too unruly, twirling and tripping by like autumn leaves, like the girl's ridiculously curly hair that is too long and curls towards the small of her back when she is naked.

Her impossibly white back, freckled and firm.

Oh, he says, stupidly. I should call the guys before it's too late and make sure everything went OK while I was gone. And I'd like to get home before dark to check on ... things.

Sure, his wife smiles.

Breathe.

Smell the small triumph.

The waiter removes the steak. The man swallows another glass of red wine without tasting it.

He holds her little hand in his, the hand he has been married to for thirty years.

Great, he says. I can't wait to call her. A baby. Great.

Later yet, the girl still sleeping, he calls her from the greenhouse and lets the phone ring until the machine picks up, lets her voice make its announcement, hangs up.

His finger severs the connection.

In the darkness, the seedlings glow green in their trays, stretching as far as the eye can see, dozens of different species, under the ineffectual fraction of a winter moon.

The season persists.

The walk back to the house looks endless, the ground frozen and slick. Ice crystals dangle from the eaves. Icicles.

Exhale.

A cloud of frozen breath hangs heavy in the air. It's hard to breathe when it is this cold, when the mercury drops this low. The trees stand strong, unscathed, unaffected.

Their roots reach down to the warm heart of the earth.

A baby. His daughter is having a baby. (His son, Steven, has three children. Yet, this is different. His little girl.)

Slowly and surely he feels himself being pulled back into the heart of his family. The roots he has planted reach around his throat and tighten.

Restlessness.

The earth is restless. A wind is building far in the north, capturing snow to carry down. Capturing ice to wrap around this family. If he struggles, it will only hold him tighter.

Derek has not slept all week. When he shuts his eyes at night he is overwhelmingly aware of the patterns on the back of his eyelids, the strange shapes that float by. He can't see as far as sleeping because all this is in his way.

When he does sleep, his dreams take him out onto a frozen lake where faces mock him from under foot. His dreams break the ice with a shattering glass sound and force him awake with the shock of water, frozen.

Alone.

His lover has left him, maybe, or perhaps has just drifted away. He has been gone for days, or longer. Weeks. Derek cleans the kitchen floor. Again. He hunches over the tile, inhales the bleach, thinks, what did I do? Where did I go wrong? He scrubs mercilessly until the cleanser begins to sting his knuckles. Red raw flesh that pulls and tugs when he moves his fingers.

He allows himself to cry.

Look:

Outside, white flakes are pouring from the dark sky like coconut, swirling into the darkness.

The flakes glow from within, making the darkness into half-light. All that pure cold snow begins to coat the ground. Soon, it will be deep, then deeper. Inches, feet.

Such a blanketing of the earth must muffle sounds, like hearts breaking.

The wife lies awake in her husband's arms. His sleeping erection presses against her buttocks. Nudges.

Are you having another affair?

The girl hops clumsily to the bathroom and has to put drops of saline in her eyes in order to peel off her forgotten contact lenses. In the mirror, her eyes stare back, dry and papery and red. It is always so cold in this apartment. The tile is painful beneath her feet.

Seek warmth.

She strips down to nothing and showers, then, still chilled, fills the bath with hot sudsy water and lies in it until she can see the bright orange light of the winter sunrise. Her blackened ankle hangs over the side, still throbbing and useless. The room is silent except for the steady dripping of the tap. The mirror is thick with steam. She feels a hundred years old, thinks that if she looks in the mirror a wrinkled hag will be staring back. She swirls the water around with her hands, and the cooling surface mixes with the hot gushing from the tap. Her feet and fingers are raisin-puckered. Her foot swells in the heat, and the purplish bruising seeps up her leg like an unsightly stain.

Harry, she thinks.

When she sees bruising, purple black green yellow, she thinks of Harry.

One fist, upraised, can change everything.

Boyfriend.

Husband.

Nothing.

One fist.

He never struck her. Then, they married.

Who would believe her? Lucy, clinging to Harry's leg. Lift me up! Higher! she signed in his language. I want to touch the ceiling! I want to touch the sky!

The twins composed a piece for Harry. When the girl heard it for the first time, she could not understand why it was not full of crashing cymbals, heavy drums. Then she remembered, of course, it was only her beneath the fist. Alone. The twins were learning sign language, too.

There was something about Harry that made everyone want to learn.

Communication is very important.

His hands were giant, silhouetted against the bright bare bulb.

His anger vibrated through the room, making the curtains

tremble.

She's coming over this afternoon, the wife announces over breakfast.

The man has been far away. His eyes staring out the window at the thick snow, weighing dangerously down on the branches of young trees. His eyes have been watching the saplings, but his mind has been full of the bony protrusions of the hipbones of the girl, the way her mouth tasted in the morning before she brushed her teeth, the way he carried her from bed to bath, the way she looked at him.

Are you listening?

What?

She's coming this afternoon. Before the snow gets too bad.

She is?

Don't look so afraid.

What are you talking about?

Jamie. She's coming home. I should make up the room. I wonder if they'll need a ride from the airport. We should call, don't you think?

I don't know. I guess. Yes. You call. I have work to do.

Look outside, at the trees bending and straining under the weight of the season. Look how they bow their heads in defeat.

Lumps form on their trunks, to protect the seasonal scars of missing limbs, broken branches.

Lumps form in throats, to protect the scars. Tears, sorrow, joy.

Jamie, laughing. Jamie, learning to walk. To talk. To ride a bike. To plant a tree. To crossbreed hybrids. Jamie, planting her own forest.

How did this happen?

All grown up with the seed of her strange husband swimming around her belly, fat and happy in her womb. A baby. It didn't seem so strange when his son became a father. But his daughter, that's a different story. So young and lovely and blonde, he imagines the balloon of her childlike belly. His back curves under the meaning of the years.

I wonder if she'll want her old bike, he says.

Her bike?

The little red one, remember?

The baby isn't even showing yet.

I know. I was just ... never mind.

He eats his toast, remembers his little girl wobbling around the long driveway on one training wheel, listing dangerously to one side.

Does everyone remember their life this way? Little snippets of film from a family album, first day of school, first missing tooth, first words, first steps, first Christmas, first wedding, first baby. A lifetime of firsts.

We're getting old, he says to the back of his widening wife. How did this happen?

But she is already gone. Gone down the hall to make up a fresh bed for her daughter and son-in-law.

She is already gone.

The man will have to be careful. He is almost alone.

The girl struggles out of the tub, any weight on her ankle causing stars to drift lazily across her field of vision. Damn, she curses. Shit. Fuck. Damn. The room is empty and no one hears. She feels angry. She wants to feel angrier. She wants to feel the pressure of rage building inside until it propels her to do something. Do anything.

She channels the anger into working, forcing out a short story so vitriolic it makes her cringe. Writes a benign article about the sharks in the Farallon Islands, feeding off the seals and sea lions. Tries half-heartedly to pitch it to an editor she knows. Nothing. No sale.

Nothing. Her ankle throbs.

She hates to write. Her bank account is shrinking.

Writing is all she knows.

She goes into the tiny kitchen and puts the kettle on to make tea, watches as the steam begins to rise. The paint is bubbling off the wall above the stove. Underneath the white, patches of canary-yellow are beginning to show.

She hates yellow.

The man has not called.

Why?

Outside the snow swirls down in slow circles.

She takes the teapot downstairs, gingerly putting weight on her damaged foot. She can walk without crutches.

Her body is healing.

Alice is wigless. Her short spiky brown hair looks slept on. Her glasses, crooked on her nose, have had some sort of accident — tape holds them together at the bridge and on the arm. She looks like a teacher. A librarian. Except for the silicone breasts, of course, standing out in front of her like jungle animals stalking prey.

Lucy plays around the living room, talking to herself. The train goes over the bridge, the people on the train see rabbits, hello say the rabbits, it is almost Christmas, you must be going to the north pole to help Santa, yes say the people that is where we are going, toot toot says the train. The child's delighted laugh makes the room warmer and homier than it really is, with its threadbare couch and tweed curtains blocking out all vestiges of light.

What happened to your foot? This said through the eternal cloud of blue smoke. Blue smoke that stains the walls yellow, the sheets yellow, the curtains yellow.

I fell, in California.

California?

Did some work there on the weekend.

Lucky.

Lucky?

You're free.

Free?

Yeah. Stop echoing me. I feel like I'm in the Grand Canyon, for crissakes.

Sorry. I just don't know if I'm lucky.

Sure, you're alone. Don't have to answer to anyone. She nods towards the child. You know?

I guess. The girl coughs, the smoke settling in her lungs like mucus. Hey, you want me to take her out in the snow? To play?

You want her?

Sure.

You sure?

I said I was.

In the snow, the girl leaves a strange trail of one footprint, one toe print, and two round holes. The crutches are a burden.

Lucy is bubbling over with play, here a snow angel, there a tiny, crumbling snowman.

Snow comes from Santa's beard, she says, wisely.

Oh?

Yup. So he's invisible on Christmas. He makes it all white so we can just see his red suit if we close our eyes real hard.

Of course.

Look at Lucy dancing through the falling snow. Watch.

The girl drops the crutches and rolls snow into balls. The snowman grows.

They go to the mall, and the girl lets Lucy sit on Santa's knee.

That wasn't the real Santa, the child announces in disgust.

No? How can you tell?

He smelled funny.

Funny?

The real Santa smells like cookies.

What did this one smell like?

Like funny old hairspray. Stinky! She plugs her nose, and falls to the ground laughing. Laughing until tears squirt out her eyes. Not like cookies!

The girl lets Lucy roll around on the floor until she is finished. Her arms ache and her foot swells out of the confines of the bandage. They take a cab home, the child keeping up a steady monologue out the window. I want a Barbie for Christmas, a pretty Barbie with black hair. Why is Barbie blonde? Black is better. Why is it so cold? Does it have to be cold for snow? I hope it snows forever. I wish it was warm. Do you think Momma will have lunch ready?

It is three o'clock in the afternoon, the girl realizes that she is not hungry, nor has she eaten today. She sighs.

Sure, she says. I'm sure she'll have lunch.

Back in the apartment she remembers to check her messages. Her sister. The editor calling back to say he'll take the piece but it needs to be shorter by at least a hundred words.

Methodically, she rewrites the piece, then calls her sister back and listens to the busy signal beep in her ear.

The room is quiet and pale, empty. The twins are obviously out because there are no sounds of music, only the hushed roar of traffic, muffled by the fresh snow. She tries to remember what she used to do, before. Before she started waiting for the man to call, before she knew the man.

Was there anything before?

Of course, there is only one thing. One obvious thing she used to have.

She used to have Harry.

She remembers how his presence in the room started to feel suffocating, like a hand around her throat.

Harry didn't believe in love. Or so he said. Even in their wedding vows, the word love was unspoken.

Why did she marry him?

She clears her throat, Harry. Harry, she said. Harry.

Harry.

He doesn't look up, because of course he can't hear her. Besides, he is scrambling eggs intently. Ground pepper, chopped onion, celery, cheese. Helps himself, ignoring her, ignoring the blossoming blue-black-purple of her eye.

Harry, she says, banging the table so that his plate jumped.

And he looks up.

Harry, she says. Get out.

What?

She knew he could see. That was the thing with Harry. He might not be able to hear you, but he could look at your lips and your eyes and your hands and know exactly, within a shadow of a doubt, what you were thinking in your heart.

He looks up at her. What?

But he knows. He must know. So smart, Harry is. Eternal university student. Going to school for free on the government dime.

Harry and his damn sharks.

She leaves the room and goes into the living room, curls herself onto the couch with her back to the door, falls asleep that way, sleeps all that day and night, dreams of Harry's back receding in the distance, dreams of Harry running away, walking away, climbing down the steps, driving away. When she wakes up he is gone. All his things are gone.

He leaves a note. Jagged letters scrawl across unopened mail.

It says:

I was going to go anyway.

The fact of her aloneness stretches around the room and ricochets, a rubber bullet of herself.

Alone.

The man loves her.

Didn't he use that word?

The room smells of smoke and burning wood. Heat crackles behind the grate. Jamie sits perched on the arm of the sofa, leaning into her husband, Dylan. Dylan is a pilot. He frequently does this run so he can visit her parents, weaving himself inextricably into the fabric of the family. The man used to think this was nice, that this made them stronger. Now he resents it. Resents the intrusion, resents the family.

Dylan brought his wife this time as a celebration. The man

frowns. Dylan's wife. His baby. Jamie looks the same to him as she always has, like his little girl.

The wife rushes around with drinks and food.

The girl does not exist here.

What do you think, Dad? If it's a boy, we'll name him after you?

Really?

The power of family draws tighter around his windpipe. Swallow. He takes another long sip of Scotch.

His daughter leans over and says, you're looking so well, Dad, so young, tell us, what is the secret?

It is only when she says this that he thinks of the girl, the tilt of her pelvis as she rides him slowly, the glow of her tears in the moonlight. Clichés. Everything is a cliché.

Family, he answers. You keep me young. He strokes his daughter's soft blonde hair, his hand catching in a hairsprayed curl. You'll see, he says. You'll see when your own daughter is born.

Do you think it's a girl?

Of course!

The conversation rises and swells around the smell of the hot food and fire and the man allows himself to sink into the quicksand of contentment.

He will call the girl later.

Later he will see her.

Later.

In her apartment, the girl is seeing ghosts: everything she looks at appears in duplicate. The table has another table behind it. The sofa, another sofa. The window, anther window. She watches the cars drive by, their headlights glowing double on the wall.

Oh my God, she thinks. I am going crazy.

She shuts her eyes, and her thoughts are doubled. Her head aches like her ankle, the pain not seeming to know where in her body to stop.

Sip again another punishing swallow of Scotch. Scotch was the drink her father favoured. We all become our parents, she mumbles. She laughs a little. Maybe that was funny.

Her parents in the car, pills spilling over the vinyl seats onto the floor.

When the man finally calls to say he can't come over, she is almost asleep. His voice comes to her over the sound of background chatter. She can hear his wife. He is whispering.

You're going to get caught, she taunts. Watch out for the wife.

I don't care, he says, so quietly she can't hear.

Doesn't matter anyway, she adds, I have other plans.

Liar.

Purge.

She begins sorting through her cupboards to keep herself busy, recycling all the scraps she has kept for so long.

Throw away the sculptures. Is this progress?

The black glaze is smooth under her fingers. Cold. One figurine breaks against the other, and she fishes out only that one from the pile of trash, the two broken pieces making her cry. Glue it back together. She cradles the pieces of her own pubescent body in her hands, until the pieces set, well after midnight.

Why does she feel so awful?

The girl is in love.

The girl is drunk with Scotch and love and loneliness.

She dreams about a woman in a tiny blue car, driving down the highway, pinned to the earth when an aeroplane is forced down on a cold, winter night, forced to land on what at first looked like a deserted road, the tiny blue car causing the plane to tip too much to one side, causing the gas to spill out on the road, the cigarette that the woman has just thrown out the window causing the earth to explode.

She awakens sitting straight up on the couch.

Has she slept?

For the first time in years, the man makes love to his wife, realizing that with his glasses off, and in the dark, she is still the woman that he married, her soft small hands skimming over his skin like a memory.

Is that significant?

Watch:

Harry buys a lover in Japan, where they are not called hookers but something else that he can't make out because reading lips is hard enough in English. He tries to make love to her, his giant body dwarfing her. He tries to make her hips move.

Her lips keep moving, she keeps talking. And he can't. He just can't. He tries to touch her skin to see if the smooth almond flesh will help him, but it doesn't.

Her lips flap loosely like a rock cod, bulging and wet. He smells the salt of the sea, turns his back to her. The bed vibrates with her voice.

He reaches over. His giant hand floats towards her. Settles on her flapping fish lips, tightens. Only then can he find satisfaction. Only then, his hand clamped over her voice.

He doesn't hear her leave, but later, when he opens his eyes, he is aware of the empty space on the bed behind him and he is relieved.

So much talking makes it hard to listen.

Drive.

The snow has been pushed off roads with ploughs, salted and sanded. Gritty pavement is spat out behind his tires.

So many lies.

Drive, climb the stairs. Don't stop and listen to the music floating ephemerally through closed windows. Don't look in.

Knock. Don't knock. Use the key, hidden so obviously under

the mat.

The man bursts into the room, his hands already all over the girl's body, pushing her against the wall. Aroused, yet still half asleep, she allows him to turn her over, enter her from behind, violent, skirting on the edge of pain. Allows him to do whatever he needs to do, slipping and sliding around the sleep she so recently left, her body becoming only an extension of him as he searches so hard for his pleasure. He pushes her legs this way and that.

Is this love?

Afterwards, they lie breathless in the tangle of blankets.

Your apartment is a mess, he observes.

Yes.

Looking for something?

Just throwing things away.

What things?

Oh, junk. Nothing important.

I couldn't call. Family stuff. Are you angry?

She shrugs. Whatever.

I thought of you. All day.

You did?

All day. The lies come to this man so easily, sharks gliding dangerously through the water.

He continues: Do you have any pictures?

Pictures of what?

Of you.

Me?

When you were a child.

No.

No? I thought your parents were gone. You have no pictures?

No. Why would you ask that?

I want to know you. Know all about you. I want to know what you were like as a little girl.

Why?

I don't know. Aren't you curious about me?

Some parts of you. She drops her hand down between his legs, caressing so gently he is reminded of butterfly wings and leaves stirring in the wind.

Later, she goes outside and sits on the porch, despite the cold. No new snow has fallen, but yesterday's velvet whiteness still covers every surface. It occurs to her that in winter there are very few smells. Spring and summer smell green and fresh — lawn clippings and new growth. Fall smells damp and like the earth itself. But winter, there is snow. Unscented cold air. Nothingness.

The girl has no pictures of herself as a child because she has thrown them all away. There were hundreds. Thousands.

The girl's father is a photographer. A camera always in his hand, his hand that always smells like darkroom chemicals. He wins awards. Publishes books. Has gallery shows.

Her father is famous. The girl is famous in pictures, a grim-faced elfin child with awkward haircuts (that photograph well). She is never smiling in the prints.

Her father kills himself, almost, and she throws away the pictures. He would be angry if he knew. The pictures were worth money. She can't throw away all of them, they exist in books, calendars, posters.

Her father almost kills himself, and in so doing kills the girl in the pictures. She disappears. The plane crashes into the earth, killing everyone, on the plane, on the ground.

She stops going to school on picture day, faking sickness.

There are no more pictures.

This is why her sister has never forgiven her.

How strange, she thinks, that the man would ask to see them.

The cold snow feels good on her ankle, but her lips and nails begin to turn blue. It is only then that she goes back inside, fills the tub with hot water, sinks under the surface with gratitude for the heat and the steam. Thinking of the man, she touches herself gently until she comes again. Warm. Sleepy.

It occurs to her that the only time she feels good, feels really healthy and alive and good, is during sex, at the moment of orgasm, when she floats so far from her body that she ceases to exist.

Chapter 6

Harry follows the white shadows through the oceans of the world.

The plane floats dreamily down on the tarmac, cutting through the shimmering skin of heat.

Australia. The Great Barrier Reef. Harry is running out of money. His grant is withering away. This is his last chance.

Ever?

Maybe.

He has made arrangements to go out on a biological expedition. He has made arrangements to go down in the cage.

Everything has a price.

His heart beats hot and fast. The great white shark. The master.

He may be able to reach out and touch the prehistoric king of the sea. Maybe.

Harry does not know fear. Only awe. He has studied this beast for years, knows the facts. The scientific facts. The bite and spit theory. The moveable jaw. The teeth that grow and grow again. The size, the immutable size. The beauty. He can tell you the Latin name. Identify the shark from blurred shadow in a photograph. He can tell you how many are killed by people each year.

He can write books.

But he has never seen one, in the flesh. Never experienced one.

Not yet.

Jamie pulls the man aside.

Dad?

Yes.

We're on our way.

Oh?

We'll be back at Christmas, of course.

Of course.

Dad?

Yes?

I was talking to Derek and ...

Huh.

Dad. God. Listen, I'm trying to tell you something. To ask you.

Sorry.

He said Steven asked him ...

Asked him what?

I don't know how to say this, Dad.

What is it?

You're not having another affair, are you?

Winter becomes a vacuum. An endless grey sky. An eternal season.

The man flinches, as though struck. His daughter wavers in front of him, blonde and pink cheeked. Eyes wide.

Another affair?

He turns his back on his daughter. Begins the slippery walk down the driveway towards the greenhouses.

Turns his back.

Everywhere he looks, there they are.

Are you having another affair?

His wife's paintings mock him from the walls. Stacked so carelessly.

What has he done? He dials the girl's number, his fingers moving automatically as if they have a mind of their own. Hangs up. Dials again.

I'm coming over, he says. I'll be right there.

At the bottom of the street, the truck slides out from under him and into the stop sign, in slow motion. A gentle bang. The sign bends gently to the ground, bowing. The truck shudders and stops.

In the silence, his heart thunders.

He sits for several minutes, looking at his own tracks in the snow. Gets out of the truck and walks the eternal driveway back to the house.

Back home.

Did anyone notice he was gone?

Derek's coming over to help with the Christmas trees, his wife says. Steven isn't sure if he'll be able to make it down. The snow. She shrugs.

The roads are slippery.

He nods, and sinks into his chair by the fire, the glowing embers of the Scotch in his hand warm the pit of his belly. Wants to sit there forever. Wants to call the girl. Wants to never call again.

Sometimes she weeps during orgasm.

His heart thuds hard against his chest.

Dial.

The truck wouldn't start.

Oh.

So I can't come.

I know, that's OK. I'm pretty tired.

Do you miss me?

Of course.

Do you love me?

Yes.

What?

Sorry?

I didn't hear you.

Oh, it was nothing. Will I see you tomorrow?

My daughter is pregnant.

Congratulations. I guess. Grandpa.

Don't call me that, it makes me old.

Would you be any younger if you had no grandchildren?

No. You make me young.

Sorry? There was static, I couldn't hear.

That's OK. Go to sleep. Sweet dreams.

The man sits on the edge of the bed, his head in his hands. Love, he thinks, despairingly, love. He can feel the heaviness in his groin, the pull of the girl.

Come in here, he calls to his wife. Let's see what two old grand-parents can do.

Twice in two days.

Are you having another affair?

Is this all we are ever going to talk about?

Sometimes the force of love compels people to act out of character.

The girl braids her hair tightly against her scalp. Her white face stares back from the mirror, eyes dark as death. Angry. She limps down the stairs, pillowy soft under the inches of snow.

The snow.

Where are you going in this weather? The twins appearing in their doorway like magic. T-shirts and shorts, oblivious to the cold.

Oh, out. I have to go somewhere.

Where?

Visiting. I have to go. Really.

Take our car, they say. Please. It has chains.

Really?

Of course.

She knows when they look at her they see Harry. What did he do to make them love him, she wonders. What could Harry possibly have done?

She accepts the keys, gently. Holds them as though they might shatter if she closes her grip.

The tire tracks roll out behind her, pronounced. The chains are noisy, cutting through the snow. She goes carefully. Once on the highway, she moves faster, the chains rattling against the ploughed pavement. Faster and faster.

The back roads are more dangerous.

She has not visited the farm since the interview, a lifetime ago.

Is this real, or is she dreaming?

She drives through the glacial grey-white landscape with the headlights off, her way lit by the glowing snow. Snow-white. White light.

His truck is nestled up against the stop sign on the corner. She doesn't stop and look. She doesn't stop.

She cannot stop.

A line has been crossed.

No lights. The chains crinkle against the gravel. Crash against the crushed rock. Up the driveway to the darkened house.

Watch the girl:

Getting out of the car, stealing around like a burglar, peering in the windows, limping through the snow. She sees a dying fire. She sees an empty room. She sees furniture and shapes. There are no sounds, no music. She sees the criss-crossing of tracks on the driveway.

She is scaring herself.

Why is she here?

She half-hops, half-runs back to the car. A strange set of tracks is left behind, incriminating. One footprint, one toe print.

She rolls down the driveway with the engine off, stealing away like a thief in the night.

Can this be true?

She falls asleep in the car, parked beside the man's truck at the stop sign, as close to him as she can get. Falls asleep for at least an hour, or maybe more, waking only to the sound of her own shivering in the hollow echo of a silent night.

She is home before the dawn breaks, home before anyone knows the difference.

Harry turns his face up to the sun. The heat of the dock feels good and strong and pure through the rubber soles of his shoes. The water is impossibly blue. He approaches the boat, his footstep soundless. People mill around, tanned and shirtless. Supplies are being loaded. Harry adds his camera bag to the pile and begins heaving things on board. His muscles ripple, glisten. People talk to him and he smiles politely.

He points to his ear.

Deaf, he says in an earthquake roar.

People stop what they are doing to look.

The girl awakens in another white cold dawn and sees another day, aware only that she can't run and that her muscles must be atrophying and she is dying inside, like a candle burnt down to a nub, sinking into darkness. Something has to end.

She refuses to remember her drive last night.

Hello? (Please come over, she is saying, but silently, in her head. Please come over now.)

I don't know if I can get away today, he is saying. His voice is muffled. His family must be around. Derek's coming this afternoon. We have to get the rest of the trees shipped into town. They aren't going to sell out here. They're already cut. We have to bring them in.

Oh.

I'll call tomorrow.

(Tomorrow and tomorrow and tomorrow.)

Empty day.

The girl has nothing left to clean.

All around her, white surfaces reflect the bare bulbs' glare.

Inside, outside.

A distraction is necessary:

She watches talk shows, abysmal, pathetic — flipping back and forth between the outcries of man's inhumanity to man. Now is the winter of our discontent, she thinks, watching students who beat up their teachers, teachers who practice voodoo, wives who have placed curses on their husbands, men who cheat.

Oh?

She watches the men who cheat. None of them mention love. Sex. Only sex.

Next.

The channels flick by. Movie stars. Infomercials. Cartoons.

Downstairs she can hear Alice yelling at Lucy. Do not draw on the walls! How many bloody times to I have to goddamn tell you, you little brat! Jesus Christ!

She closes her eyes.

The violins sing.

Lucy cries.

Maybe this is why she answers the phone when it rings (always ringing, demanding her attention), answers the call and agrees in a voice not her own but one that belongs to a teenager she doesn't remember being, to have lunch with some girls from her high school who are in town for a convention. Multilevel marketing.

Horrors!

Do people still do this? Have lunch?

This is a normal thing to do. Nothing is normal. She must pretend to be normal.

The girl dresses carefully. She hasn't forgotten high school, the pressure to dress to perfection. Black turtleneck, expensive jeans, black boots. Cashmere coat. The girl owns these clothes, for occasions just like this. Gold earrings. Perfume, makeup. She is so thin, her jeans hang off her bones.

High school was a lifetime ago.

The restaurant is busy and over-crowded. People escaping the slushy brown snow.

The girl does not see the wife and her son over in the corner, so far away, the son making the mother laugh with some story told with flamboyant arm gestures. Even when a soup bowl crashes to the floor, and the son begins to sob on his mother's shoulder, the girl does not notice. After all, the sound in the restaurant is deafening, servers and clients all caught up in the clamour of activity.

Her high school friends have put on weight.

Immediately:

How have you *been?* What have you been *up* to? Are you married yet? Tell us everything.

She can hardly fathom their white dimpled faces, carefully curled bangs, hairspray lacquered ponytails — the Dion quintuplets.

She calls them by the wrong names.

They stare.

Not much, she says, staring into the empty white cavern of the ceiling. You?

Pregnancy and typing jobs and Prozac and their dogs and cats and other people from school and the girl flinches, thinking: God, I do not belong here. She is there in the restaurant, but she is thinking of the man and the way his fingers trace the contours of her leg, how they dig into the warmth behind her knee, in the crook of her elbow. She thinks of how his face looks below hers, how love looks.

She is separate from this gaggle of girls, she is floating up in the expanse of the ceiling.

She doesn't know them.

She doesn't care.

God, she says, so suddenly that they all stop yammering and look up. God. I'm sorry, I just remembered. I have an appointment. An interview. It's really important. God. How stupid.

They stare at her departing back.

Weird, she hears them say. What's with her? She's way too thin. Strange. Do you think she's sick?

Their voices gradually recede into the din.

She stops at the first phone booth, calls the man.

I have to see you.

I told you, I can't. Not today.

Please ...

My wife ...

Is she home?

No. He sighs. I have a few hours. She's at lunch, then shopping. I think that's what she said. But Derek ...

Yes?

He's coming, soon.

Oh.

It's OK, he says. Come anyway.

They go into his office, where they first met. There is an awkwardness that trips their tongues. Slowly, they come together. Kissing. Unsure. The warm heady smell of pine and cedar and peat moss and wet dirt mingling with the hot stench of sex. The awkwardness gives way to a jerky urgency. Desperate. The girl traces the outlines of his scars with her tongue. What's this one from? Car accident. And this one? Slipped in the creek. And this one here? Hacksaw.

A lifetime of battle scars.

An hour. Two.

Bodies sliding together, slick with sweat.

There is a knock on the glass door, a thousand miles away. He'll go away, says the man after a pause. Then, he'll be back.

The man lets down his guard for a second and is lost in the iron muscle of the girls smooth thigh, the hot red flower of her lips.

The man is lost, don't you see?

He didn't have a chance.

Out the window, they watch Derek make his way carefully down to where the men are bundling the trees for transport. Their cheeks are red from the wind, eyes watering. He disappears into their midst.

Afterwards:

I want to see your house, she says, simply.

The man looks at his watch, estimates the amount of time before his wife will be home. They walk up to the house, she steps carefully on one foot and then on one toe.

Does he recognize the tracks?

Have you been here before?

Yes. Of course. The interview. Or don't you remember?

Of course I remember, it was the best day of my life.

But that isn't what he meant. Her footprints crunch into the frozen snow.

Have you ever come here at night?

Questions prowl unasked and unanswered.

They hold hands like school children, and every once in a while she grabs on to his arm, apologetic. He sees the ripples of pain around her eyes and says absently, you should probably see a doctor about that foot.

Just a sprain, she shrugs. It will heal itself. In time.

Time heals all wounds.

Time wounds all heels.

He leads her quickly through the house, glancing nervously at his watch the whole time, purposely avoiding the bedroom. Her eyes take in the colours, the wood beams, the elaborate carpentry, the scads of photos of the kids growing up. The photos of the man and his wife. The smell that his wife must leave in each room, lavender or toothpaste. When he is getting her a drink in the kitchen, she peers into the master bedroom and sees them there, bodies entwined, the man and his wife.

What is this?

Guilt?

No.

Jealousy.

Everywhere pictures, smiling pictures, gazing off every flat surface.

You have a lovely family, she says, in a strange formal little voice. Very pretty.

Her hands brush against his when he passes her the drink, she feels the tingling of flesh on flesh, his coarse callused hands, hers smooth and unmarked. She does not imagine the tingling. The man looks at her hands, I wish I were thirty years younger, he says to her fingers.

But I'm not, he says in his mind, turning back into the kitchen, everywhere the image of his wife. Goddamnit, I'm not.

My daughter is pregnant, he says, smiling.

I know, she snaps. You already told me.

It is this house.

This house is trapping him, keeping him away from her. When his back is turned, she takes a picture of the family from the mantel, a tiny picture, two little boys, a tiny girl, a man and his wife. She steals it so quickly, she is not even sure that she has done it.

You know what? she asks suddenly. I have to go. I just remembered.

She doesn't wait to say goodbye. All the way home the tiny frame pokes into her leg through her pocket, reminding her of what she has become.

Derek hears a car starting up the hill, and cranes his neck to see. The trees are an impenetrable curtain. He shrugs, goes back to his task. The trees bundled tightly with string like a straitjacket, piling up in the back of the truck.

Massacre.

He gets a satisfaction from the massacre of his father's trees.

The girl stops at the side of the road and throws the photo into a clearing. The glass breaks as it hits the frozen earth. Could she be that strong? It lies, face down, in defeat.

The old snow is partly melting, partly frozen into sheets. Driving is treacherous, but still, the wife inches her way to the hospital, armed with the thick wool scarves. She has woven patterns into these scarves: falling snow, green trees. The outdoors that these boys will never see again, reduced as they are to their final forms, bones on which some stubborn flesh still hangs, ridden with open sores. She thinks maybe the wool will muffle the coughing, the incessant coughing that shakes her so deeply. Not my son, she prays, humming in the interminable winter silence, traffic muffled by snow. Not my boy.

Remember:

When he went on a camping trip alone with his father for the first time, so afraid he was to be away from her. But he did not let his father see him cry, no sir. A small boy marching stoically beside his strong daddy, teach me daddy, teach me how to fish and build a fire, how to cook beans that taste so good. Came back covered with mosquito bites like measles, biting his lip to keep from sobbing. Daddy and me caught a fish, he said, so proud. So small. And now, now what. Falling in love with men, ripe with death and disease. Why? Not my son, she prays, out of habit, her car steering itself towards the hospital.

Sometimes, she sees the boys' fathers come to visit, come to play cards with their sons, come to hold their sons' hands, come to say goodbye. Would her husband do that? Would he? Will he, if it comes to this?

Is he the only one who would stay away from his own dying boy?

The girl lies between white cotton sheets, looking at the stark nothingness of her apartment, the white on white on white on white, and wonders if she could go blind from all the white, which suddenly seems dazzling and strange and much too bright. When the man calls, she makes her demand, a small one, really, to him. What is it to him? Nothing. When the man calls, his voice filling up the receiver, she hears her own voice, issuing demands. You must, her voice says. You have to.

All right, the man says. Sure.

Has he heard her properly?

I won't be home, adds the girl. I'll have to see you later. I have an appointment.

Good, says the man, the doctor should look at that ankle.

The boys in the greenhouse help him load the trees into the truck, three small pines, three small firs, two blue spruce. None over five feet tall, all in pots.

He warned the girl that they will want to be planted in the ground in the spring, they may not survive long inside. The roots will become bound. The pots will strangle them.

I know, she said, sharply. What do you think? That I didn't know?

Spring will never come.

The girl is in town meeting with an editor, she is pitching another shark piece. People like to read about sharks. It's a universal fascination. She hears her own voice, smooth and intelligent, outlining the story. She sounds like an adult.

It will be a long piece.

The oceans are getting warmer, the great whites are coming farther and farther north. It's compelling.

El Niño. People want to read about it.

They hash out the details, the deadlines. He makes the agreement to her breasts, but looks her in the eye when he asks her to lunch. There is something vaguely repulsive about the way he smiles.

No, she says, I have work to do.

Research.

She sits hunched over in the library, shivering. Thinks of all Harry's shark books. All his research papers. Harry, again. She uses the Internet terminal to access as much current information as she can find. Sharks swim by jerkily on the screen.

She reads until the words blur and jump into double, then she knows it is time to stop, the information pouring through her like fresh spring water.

Limping down the street, she is weighted down with papers and books. Her laptop computer smashes against her hip. Keep moving. She limps towards a main road, where she is likely to be able to catch a bus home. Home is only twenty blocks away.

How did she become this tired?

Her foot will never heal.

The man is in her apartment.

He places trees around the white rooms while Derek waits in the truck.

Special order, he explains. It's a favour for a friend.

What friend? Derek wonders, staring up at the decaying house. Who?

Around the white rooms, the man carefully places the trees. Living room, bedroom, kitchen, bathroom. So much green. Green against white.

A sound.

Who's there?

Who are you, Lucy shouts from the doorway. How did you get in here?

Shh, says the man, startled. Shhh. It's a surprise. He tiptoes around with elaborate gestures. Christmas trees!

The child giggles in delight. Christmas trees! Christmas trees!

The man was always good with children.

His arms and back are aching from carrying the plants up all the stairs, a tiny pain is resting, curled up, in his heart. A panther about to spring. God, he thinks, closing his eyes. In the darkness, he reaches inside and traces the source of the pain to his chest. Tentacles reaching out to his jaw. His heart beats with elaborate rhythms, jumps and starts.

The child is running from room to room, touching her cheek to the trees. Christmas trees!

Dad?

He sits in the truck, silent.

Dad? Are you OK?

I'm fine, he says stiffly. Winded, that's all.

You should have let me carry them, Derek says quietly.

He's getting too old for this. The pain grips more firmly around his heart, choking off his breath.

Dad?

By the time they get to Emergency, he is pale, his hand shaking. I'm sorry, he says.

Wait here, says the nurse, efficiently.

The man sits in the waiting room, sweat pooling under his arms, Derek beside him. The boy reaches over and pats his father's hand; the man shakes him off. Snatches his hand back like he has touched something foul. Derek recedes into himself.

Old bastard, he thinks.

Once safely in the curtained enclosure, the man feels the pain floating away. Gone.

Electrodes are attached to his chest. He watches, fascinated.

A young woman enters the room, clipboard held in front.

Hello.

Are you the nurse?

No. The doctor.

Really?

The doctor is younger than his daughter.

The man feels a sinking in his gut.

After all, the chest pain is diagnosed as heartburn, probably. Or angina, maybe. Regardless, it is gone. He is to see his regular doctor, at some later time. It is not an emergency, after all.

You can't be too careful at your age.

The man leaves the hospital, a dozen years older, a bottle of antacid in his jacket pocket. Heartburn.

Don't you dare tell your mother, he hisses to Derek. I mean, I don't want her to worry.

Whatever, says Derek, sighing.

No fool like an old fool, he thinks.

The streets are slippery, festive, and crowded with bundled people rushing from shop to shop. For refuge, the girl slips into the tattoo parlour.

For refuge? No, that isn't true.

She has planned this. Noted the address. Found the shop on the map.

Something is slipping away, and she needs to grasp hold of it before it is completely gone. The man is hers. She must be marked.

The girl goes into the tattoo parlour, with purpose. The room is warm, a woman sits at the desk reading a magazine. It is not until the girl is fully in the shop that she sees this young pretty woman is sitting in a bulky red wheelchair. She had been expecting a fat man, bearded. Hell's Angels.

Expect the unexpected.

Help you?

Yes.

Well?

I need a tattoo.

Well, you come to the right place.

The girl follows the rolling chair into the back room. The drawing is discussed, created on paper. Corrected. Not quite like that, like this. Not that small. Bigger. It has to be bigger.

Make it bigger.

The girl marvels at how much the needles hurt, and how gentle the woman's touch is. Hours pass, her skin soon numb, only the scraping feeling of ink being injected into skin.

Such an endeavour can take for ever.

You're going to have to come back to finish it off, the artist announces. You know.

Why?

Can't do this other colour today, the green. Have to wait a bit for this one to heal.

OK.

Hey, I got an idea.

Yes?

We could do it in the spring. You know, like now it's winter, no leaves?

Yes.

It's perfect.

The tattoo costs over three hundred dollars. The girl leaves the smoky room, bandages covering her back. She is nauseatingly aware of the scent of burning skin. The pain distracts her from her throbbing ankle; she is able to limp all the way home.

Breathe.

More winter air to course through the blood stream, forming barricades of ice around the warm pink lungs, carrying frosty oxygen around the heart.

Keep moving.

She half jogs, a running hop, really. Papers and laptop bruising her leg. Run, hop. The sidewalks have been salted, and they crunch and slip under her good foot. Run, hop. The air feels good and sharp and unforgiving against her flushed cheeks. It takes an hour to get home this way, run. Hop.

It feels good. Really good.

At the foot of the stairs, Lucy.

Christmas trees! she says, with glee. He brought trees! Christmas trees!

Going up the stairs, the girl trips and the child catches her.

Thanks, says the girl, you're an angel.

I know! A twinkle of something happy in the child's blue iris, a grin.

Was I ever that young, the girl wonders, is that even possible? Her memories of childhood begin with school, begin with wool uniforms and men's ties knotted tightly at the throat. Her memories are sporadic. A spelling bee. The kid next to her who threw up on her desk, causing three other children to vomit on their own — the teacher's look of despair. Visiting friends on the weekend to giggle and eat cookie dough. Her own mother, skinny and unyielding; her father, his face masked by the camera. Math done in careful rows of numbers on graph paper. Running in the playground, running around the track, running through the woods behind the school. The narrow beds in the dorms. Prayers in the morning. Was there more than this? Was there mischief?

The pictures showed her as a serious child with a funny haircut that photographed well.

Lucy is tugging at her sleeve. Hurry! Christmas trees!

There they are, the forest. Filling the apartment, the white white apartment with green smells, crushed needles and warm soil.

Oh.

The child wants to decorate, pulling on the girl's hand. Can we? Can we?

They cut out snowflakes from white paper, elaborate lacy snowflakes. Wait, thinks the girl, I remember doing this. Snowflakes falling on the windows of the dorm.

They hang the flakes on the trees, white flakes, green trees.

Christmas trees!

Swallowing two Tylenol, dry, the girl picks up the phone to call him, always calling him. When the wife answers, her voice out of breath, the girl almost chokes on the white capsules. The sound comes out a dry cough. She hangs up. Not my son! the wife thinks, with alarm. The cough. What is that, a sign? An omen? She dials her son's number with shaky fingers.

I'm fine, Ma. I have to go.

Where are you going?

I have a date, all right? I have a date.

Oh.

I know.

Bye, son.

Bye, Ma. Love you.

The man stands in the doorway to the bedroom, his solid body covered with a sweater that she knitted herself, plain navy blue, with cables. Who was on the phone?

Just the boy, his wife answers sadly. He's met someone new.

Oh God. Don't tell me. The man shakes his head with disgust. Jesus.

Don't swear. The response is automatic.

Yes, dear. I'm going out.

Where are you going?

Out. Gonna meet the guys, maybe.

Meet the guys? Thirty years, and her husband has never gone out to meet the guys.

Are you having another affair?

Marriage is so many unasked, unanswered questions, a tidal wave of unsaid words — do they ever crash down? Can people be crushed under that kind of weight?

The man drives to the girl's apartment, uninvited, unannounced. The lights of the truck blur and merge with the rush hour traffic, the honking of a thousand geese. He is thinking about Christmas, his house full of grandchildren, his sons and his daughter. Family. He is thinking of the tracings of the girl's ivory white bones, lying so close to the soft smoothness of skin, the swollen mound of her sex. His truck passes under red lights, green lights; he cannot hear the angry beeps. He is, if only for a second, mentally packing his bags. He is sweeping the young girl up under his arm, flying away with her, flying south.

But then what?

What next?

They nestle together on the couch, Scotch in hand, immersed in sweaters. Looking at the white-flaked trees in the flickering light of the fire, surrounded by the green and life and smoke and warmth. They toast each other.

An offering is made: the girl has taken a book out of the library.

Watch:

Remember, she says carefully, when you asked about pictures?

Her father's photos stare up at them from the glossy pages, an elfin child, always looking just beyond the camera. A woman so much like the girl is now, always watching the child.

My sister, the girl explains.

The pictures are all black and white, tilted.

The child close to the camera, the other girl in the distance watching. There is no frivolity on these pages, only stark truth. Black and white.

You were beautiful, says the man, simply, taking her into his arms, squeezing her against his chest. The girl leaps back with a wince.

What is it?

Oh.

Oh?

I got a tattoo. Her eyes plead for something. Understanding? Forgiveness?

A tattoo? He peels back the bandage and underneath the puffy redness he can see the fine intricate lines of the tree stretching up her spine, the branches reaching towards her ribs. Black on white. A tree in winter.

Her flesh is red and angry.

You are so beautiful, he says, and holds her on his lap to make love to her, carefully placing his fingers between the branches of the tree so as not to cause her any more pain.

Lying on the sofa as the man drives away, the girl picks up the book off the table, runs her hand over the photos. The pages are so smooth, almost like fabric, tightly woven silk. The book smells musty. On the back fly-leaf, there is a picture of her father, wearing dark glasses and a beard. The only parts of his face that are visible are his forehead and two spots on his cheek. The girl has no idea what her father looked like.

She was forced into therapy after the plane crash. Her sister was to look after her, but left her in boarding school; then, at eighteen, graduation and college. She had no parents.

Wait.

Not the plane crash, the suicide. She must stop thinking of it as a plane crash.

Those burning bits of metal had nothing to do with her parents, lying dead, bottles of pills on the dash of the car. Like Romeo and Juliet. Ugly.

Wait.

She throws the book into the fire. The glossy pages don't burn well, but smoulder into an orange heat, blue flames.

The girl spreads the papers out all over the table and loses herself in the great white sharks, swimming slowly through the warming waters, following their prey north.

CHAPTER 7

People who live on islands gravitate towards water.

It's a natural instinct.

No matter that the ground is frozen two feet down. No matter that the only signs of life are the seagulls hovering on winds of ice, disappearing at the first sign of snow.

No matter that it is winter, it is Canada, it is cold.

It is impossible to describe this kind of cold. It is a frozen dampness that steals into your heart, freezing soft tissue mercilessly.

Bundle up.

The girl's hair hangs down in a limp curtain. She layers up in black wool, taping her ankle tightly with athlete's tape, not elastic, the tape thick enough to form almost a support, almost a cast, cutting off the circulation to her toes. On her way downstairs she knocks on Alice's door, to see if Lucy will come with her.

Can she come out and play?

Boys and girls come out to play.

No answer.

There is no one home.

She makes her careful, slow way through the deep snow, snow that reaches over the top of her boots to leave a dusting of white on her black wool tights. The twins. She knocks. The music flutters, then stops.

Yes?

I was wondering ...

(What is she doing here? The identical faces stare expectantly.)

I was wondering if you guys wanted to go for a walk or something. With me. She shrugs, pretending it doesn't matter, either way.

We can't, they chorus. Then — sorry. It's practising, we have to practise.

They practise for at least six hours a day. She bites back a reply. Nods.

And so, alone.

Gets to the shore and realizes she has forgotten breakfast, last night's Scotch leaving a thick ache in her head, her hands shaking slightly, a cold sweat trickling down her spine, stinging her new tattoo. The tree wraps its branches around her more firmly. The bark bites into her skin.

Do you see?

There is an ache deep in her belly. Hunger. She makes her way over to a plush white bench, brushing off the snow until it is only hard, grey wood once again, and sinks into it, gratefully.

The sea is roaring, charcoal grey. White foam sprays and froths around the rocks. A spray of salt water, reaching up towards her, whips the snowy shore. Over the sea, the air looks huge and cavernous, the clouds so high they are only a mist, no land visible on the horizon. The wind carries the snow in drifts, virgin piles.

There is no one around but the girl and the giant grey sea. She closes her eyes and sees sharks twenty feet long, as broad as small cars, churning through the deep. Don't look. Inhaling sharply, her lungs fill with salty air. The taste lingers in her mouth.

On impulse she drops to the ground and makes a snow angel, arms and legs swinging through the white. (I remember this, she thinks. Winters spent with friends from school, snow angels on so many different suburban lawns. Was she really once a child?)

Wait:

A man is walking towards her, smiling. Need help getting up?

No, I'm OK.

He smiles, something familiar in his eyes. Something familiar in his walk.

Standing, she lists alarmingly to one side.

Are you all right?

Yes. Sorry. I forgot breakfast.

Ah. Would you? He proffers a granola bar from the depths of his pocket.

No, thanks. Oh. Maybe. Yes. Yes, thanks. The granola is crunchy and sweet. It dissolves on her tongue, carefully.

He sits beside her on the bench in companionable silence.

It's when you look at that, he gestures at the sea, that you realize how irrelevant your own existence is.

Sharks, says the girl.

What?

Out there, she gestures.

Not here. It's too cold.

No, it's true. They have been caught in Washington state. I'm serious. It's something to do with El Niño warming the water.

The man sighs. El Niño, he moans. I can't stand to hear another word.

He stands up, brushing snow from his dark wool pants. Pants that cling damply to his legs. She averts her eyes. He smiles — would you like to walk?

He helps her up and they begin to walk in the place that is usually a path, keeping the angry waves on their left. He holds her elbow.

Don't worry, he says, gravely, I'm gay.

Oh. Great.

They walk. The granola bar resting in the girl's stomach allows the shakiness to subside, leaving only a slight blurring of vision. A headache that is almost forgotten.

They stop and watch a group of people practising tai chi.

Beautiful, the man says.

When they get closer, they see that the people in the group are mostly bald, their faces puffy with the unmistakable signs of sickness. Some wear scarves to cover their baldness. Beautiful silk scarves, shot through with colour so startling it takes one's breath away.

It makes the girl think of a story she read in a newspaper.

A tiny square story, no bigger than an inch of print, too small to contain any details. It said only that a strange object, like a kite or, no, perhaps a brightly coloured scarf (of silk, or some more expensive fabric), had drifted to the ground in an industrial area, whereupon several witnesses said that it had flown around as though able to control its own flight. A construction crew stopped working to observe, and said the scarf had a light, was illuminated. Aliens, they had said. A visitation from another planet.

This was printed in the paper as though it were fact. A silk scarf visitation.

Look:

The women are dancing, cancer covered by coloured silk.

Isn't it possible, the girl thinks, that it wasn't aliens. That it could have been angels. Or God. Anything could have been hidden in a swathe of iridescent gauze.

She prefers to think of it this way, that as angels drift down towards the earth, you can see the life-giving sunlight filtering through the rich cacophony of colours, colours so bright that you are at once mesmerized and afraid. They swirl relentlessly through the weightless fabric as it is lifted, furled and unfurled, by currents of air so gentle and minute that you are not aware that they are there, you cannot feel the forces that buffet the world that you live in.

Don't you see how that is possible?

Would anybody notice?

Would you?

She used to believe in fairies. And angels.

The girl had shown the story to Harry.

He had pushed it aside, unread.

Harry was only interested in sharks. This made him completely one-dimensional.

The girl watches the angels dancing.

God, says the man beside her.

Cancer?

Yes.

The women dance in the falling snow, their shiny bald heads exposed to the fresh salt air beneath translucent silk. They look lost in themselves, as though each were the only person on earth.

Is this a dream, or is it happening?

This man is talking:

I hate to be single, he is saying. It is so lonely.

Is it?

Yes, aren't you single?

Not exactly.

No, I suppose you wouldn't be.

He's married if it makes you feel better, she tosses this off. Drifting between them like the snow.

Oh.

They walk without speaking. Suddenly, the man speaks again. Into the wind, she can hardly hear him — My father used to do that! Young mistresses! I'm sorry.

Pardon?

Sorry. His words echo flatly in the feather white flakes.

Sorry?

She turns to go, her ankle pinching despite the heavy tape. She turns to go, and he calls after her.

It was nice to meet you. I didn't get your name! Wait! I'm Derek ...

Does he say Derek, or is it just a trick of the wind?

The girl is already gone.

She limps towards home, suddenly aware.that she has no feeling in her toes. The tight wrap of tape has extinguished the path of oxygen and blood.

Derek. Of course. Who else?

He has his father's eyes.

Tonight the girl has a date. The man has promised. He will take her out, to a restaurant. Out for dinner. A date.

The dancing women wore brightly coloured parkas. Colours so hopeful against the inevitable grey sea.

I think I'll go Christmas shopping, the man announces to his wife.

What?

Christmas shopping.

You never do Christmas shopping before Christmas eve.

So? This year will be different.

He dresses carefully in an expensive cashmere sweater she has not seen before. Where did you get that?

I don't know, he says, levelly. Didn't you give it to me?

The room is filled with the scent of cologne and malevolence.

Christmas shopping? The wife is not so naive.

Is she?

Outside, the wind carries the oxygen to the girl's lungs with higher velocity. Faster. Does it move though her body at the same brisk pace? Her heart, lub dub, lub dub. Does it beat faster to accommodate?

The wife picks up the phone.

Derek?

There is no one home. The answering machine plays the "Moonlight Sonata".

Mea culpa, mea culpa, mea maxima culpa.

The girl is wearing a black dress that is long-sleeved and narrow, reaching almost to the floor. When she stands against the light, he appreciates that the fabric is opaque, that no matter how thin she becomes, her body curves gently behind the black. Under it, she wears a black slip. To cover the tattoo, she explains.

Ah, yes. The tree tattoo.

She can't cover it. The branches snake upward towards her shoulders. So much ink. When she moves, the branches undulate sexily as if in a gentle summer breeze.

Silence.

In the cab of the truck they listen to the hum of the heater. The tree embraces the girl from behind, cold and leafless, but intricate and beautiful all the same. It is strong, and can support her. They park half a block from the restaurant, one where he has never been with his wife. Obviously.

He notices that she has stuffed her swollen foot into a high black pump, backless. Don't slip, he cautions. In heels, she is taller than the man, spindly and straight. A birch, so white. An elm.

Into the womb of the restaurant, a reverse birth. Ice-cold air, to thick warm flavours. She sits with her back to the fire, gazing around the room as if looking for someone she knows. He reaches across the table and takes her hand.

Have I told you that you are beautiful?

Yes.

Ah.

Wine and gentle music. Be a child pretending to be grown up. Be a grown-up pretending to be a child. When she looks around the restaurant she sees a sea of silver hair. Even the light brown hair on the head of the man is streaked with silver in this low, heavy light.

The food is delicious. Chicken in sauce so exquisite her mouth hurts, saliva rushing to meet flavour.

This is wonderful, she says.

Yes, he says, it is. It should always be like this.

Look at the waiter:

Does he frown in disapproval? Or is he merely thinking of his own life, his own problems, holding them up against the backdrop of food and conversations?

The girl reaches across the table to kiss the man gently on the lips. Is it her imagination or does conversation stop? Is there a pause in time? She hopes they are seen by someone he knows.

Why?

He thinks of the pain he had before, in his heart. Love, he thinks, helplessly.

But still, there is always time to answer to. Hours. Minutes. What was the question?

Smell this:

The hot smell of ginger, cinnamon, nutmeg. Chocolate melting in a pan.

The Christmas baking, of course, still has to go on.

Prepare icing, affix Smarties and licorice to the cookie faces. The wife moves mechanically through the work. She misses the children. Will they be here soon? Jamie set to arrive Christmas eve. Steven coming when the weather allows him through. Derek. Where is Derek? The radio is tuned to an oldies station. I saw Mummy kissing Santa Claus, she sings, underneath the mistletoe last night.

The king is in the counting house, counting out the money. The queen is in the kitchen, eating bread and honey.

The clock drags its heavy hands towards nine o'clock.

Derek is at the movies, watching *It's a Wonderful Life*, in black and white, popcorn making a greasy spot on his carefully pressed jeans.

Alone. He looks around the crowd, the backs of so many heads. He cradles a cup of coffee between his knees.

His eyes seeking, seeking.

Such a habit! To scan the crowd for warm eyes, a beckoning smile. His gaze wanders.

Wait:

An older man, sitting slightly behind and several seats over from him. His heart hastens to catch up to his breath. The man winks, and lowers his head.

Did he really wink?

Yes, Derek thinks. Yes.

It is singles night at the theatre, a world of possibility.

The man and the girl sip coffee, slowly. Making it last.

Tell me, the man is saying, about your dreams.

My dreams? As in, what I see when I am sleeping? Or what I want to do with my life?

Both.

These are my dreams.

Pardon?

Being with you. I sleep them. I want this, when I grow up.

I wish I were thirty years younger.

Why?

So we could ...

Why can't we now? What does that mean?

I ...

What.

Can't we just have this, for now?

What is this?

Love, he thinks. But he answers: I don't know.

When he drops her off, she kisses him hard, catching his bottom lip and biting until he pulls away. She leaves lipstick on his cheek. On purpose? Yes. On purpose.

Can't we just have this, for now?

Inside, she calls her sister:

How are you?

Fine, how are you?

Good.

So.

Anything new?

No. You?

No. How are the kids?

Really good. Listen, I promised them I'd take them shopping. You know, for Christmas. To buy a surprise for Daddy, you know? Can I call you some other time?

Sure.

The girl hangs up the phone without saying goodbye. Daddy?

She wants to call the man, but she can't.

The branches sigh and move behind her. Can she feel it? The roots are taking hold.

Crashing through the girl's veins, like the angry waves on the winter sea, uncertainties swirl and reach and churn. Thirty years. The man is right, of course. There is so much more to him than to her, at twenty-three. He is life, has lived, has stories to tell. She is a child. A sex object? Perhaps.

Don't believe that, she whispers to herself. This is love.

In the spice-laden kitchen, the man approaches his wife.

I'm back!

What did you buy? (Does he notice how her voice is level and flat? Does he notice how she does not look him in the eye — instead, back to him, she scrubs mixing bowls and trays in the sink. Does he notice how the gingerbread men aren't smiling?)

Oh, nothing yet. I was just ... looking.

I see.

Does he notice how she doesn't ask any more questions?

The boat floats lazily along the calm sea. The impossibly blue sea. Harry longs to tip backwards and fall into its embrace. Sink into the blue.

These are shark waters, he has been told. Infested. The cage sits on the deck of the boat, hanging from pulleys and wire cables thick enough to lift a car. A building. The cage, waiting.

The crew members dump buckets of chum into the water. The air takes on the fetid stench of fish guts, the metallic tang of blood. Harry waits. Ready. Ready to go in at the slightest sign of activity.

For miles around, the sea is undisturbed. No other boats on the horizon. The deck glistens, sun throws daggers into his eyes. It is so hot. Hard to breathe in air so hot and humid.

He hit the girl and she left. No. He hit her, then he left. What kind of man is he? His eyes move across the surface methodically, like radar. Scanning for the familiar fin. Anything.

The first day out, they saw porpoises. Beautiful, but disappointing. Certain to be no sharks around.

Today, nothing.

On their wedding day, they were both drunk. Sad, isn't it?

Harry leans over and removes a curl of hair that is stuck to the girl's lips. They have been dancing, although it is only two. In the afternoon. The bar opened at eleven, and there they were, the only customers.

He speaks with his hands. Maybe he loves her because she can read his signs. He doesn't understand why she refuses to use them for him.

The girl gets up on the stage and sings karaoke. To him. A deaf Indian, drunk at a bar. He cringes at his own image.

It is the university bar, but a bar all the same.

The girl gyrates on the stage like a stripper.

When he claps and whistles, she bursts into tears. That's when he says: look, we should probably get married.

She doesn't even ask why. He doesn't have to say, because I love you.

In reality, he doesn't know her at all.

There is some activity at the bow of the boat. Is it true? A churning in the water. So much activity, all at once. Harry looks over the side. Adjusts his tanks, breathes. Spits in his mask. Ready?

Ready.

He fights the urge to leap into the water, cageless. Free.

He can see the jaw thrusting forward towards the bait. So huge. Bigger than he imagined, than he could have imagined.

The steel cage drops into the water with a splash and a clatter. What would the shark be thinking?

He's gone, someone shouts. It's gone.

Good thing Harry can't hear. He's already over the side, swimming for the tiny cage. His heart beats in his throat. At any moment, he expects to be lifted out of the water, held in a vise-like grip. At any moment, he expects a shark to swim by at an amazing speed. Expects to feel the current in the water, livid and real. Expects to be able to reach out and touch the flesh of the giant fish.

Inside the cage he feels like bait on a hook. Dancing around, looking everywhere at once. Camera ready.

The first blow is always unexpected.

He only hit her once, seeing as if from a distance his fist coming down towards her eye, building force. Wanting, really, to hurt her. To make her stop. To stop her lips from moving.

She wasn't the one.

He knew as soon as he saw her move underwater, awkward. In a hurry. Breathing wrong, too fast, too hard.

She wasn't the right one, that was all.

The cage swings sharply. His eyes were looking the wrong way. Imagine a jaw of teeth, so many teeth, open behind you. Laughing, smiling, soundless. The steel tremors.

Harry feels the hot rush of urine in his wetsuit.

Is this fear?

He breathes slowly. Wants to swim free of the cage, and away. The shark circles. A miracle. The shark so close.

The shutter snaps. Again and again.

From another cage, he watches another diver carefully feed

the shark with fish. Chum floats on the surface, murky red and viscous.

Better than he could have hoped, another shark joins the first. Then another. And another.

Six sharks, circling. Each twenty feet long, twenty-five. Their enormity is spectacular. Their skin is marked with scars. Charcoal-grey. White bellies. White scars. They swim above and below and all around.

Looking up towards the surface, he can see the sunlight pouring down towards him. The bottom of the boat. The steel cable.

Two sharks strike at once. He hears the vibration through his feet. The steel does not give way.

Then, they are gone.

No.

Harry lets his arms hang out the openings on the side of the cage. Come back, he signs. Please.

His tank is running low.

The grinding of the pulleys, and the cage shudders to the surface. He swims free, lingering in the water, lifting his mask. Kicking his feet.

Sharks are drawn to a struggle, movement in the water.

Harry kicks his feet.

The sharks are gone.

The sun pours into his eyes like blindness.

He only hit her once. Surely, that can be overlooked.

Chapter 8

Birds, outside her window.

Someone must have taken pity: sprinkled some seeds, crumbs, on the icy white surface. It is snowing in hard little pellets. The season is nearly depleted of beauty, white flakes giving way to grey stones. Bruising that has faded to yellow and green reaches up her leg, towards her toes. Spreading like ink under her skin. Ink over her back. She can see it if she cranes her neck, the tree, protecting her. Shading her. The detail is breathtaking.

The detail is excruciating.

Deep in her uterus, she feels the first pull of cramps, the first twist.

It is only then that she realizes that, this month, there has been no bleeding. An ache deep inside. She takes a Tylenol, two. Wills it to go to her cramp, to her belly, to her heart. How much pain can it control?

She closes her eyes and tries to conjure up spring: daffodils, tulips, green grass, children. What else? Butterflies. People wearing short-sleeved shirts as though they themselves have just burst out of a cocoon. Snow cocoon. Rain. She imagines the splatter of drops falling on the roof. Running in the rain, smelling spring and exhaust, sweat mingling with water. Rainbows. Fleshy pink skin.

Running in the rain, the smell of steaming sidewalks. Wet grass.

She must be half asleep, she can feel her heart start working harder, oxygen pumping to muscles that have not been used since California: eternal summer. Seems a lifetime ago.

Still, his words, from last night. What were they exactly? *Can't we just have this.* This?

This what?

Hate the wife. Imagine faults and fat thighs, curse her with a hormonal moustache, dimpled buttocks. Sagging breasts. Make her dull.

I miss you, she says to the non-existent man. Goddamn you all to hell.

It is Saturday morning.

From downstairs, silence.

This gives meaning to the phrase — *the silence is deafening.*

Normally, Saturday morning, the violins do battle with the roar of Lucy's cartoons. The girl frowns. Perhaps they went away. Do they have family somewhere else? She doesn't know.

Alice's husband beat her, but she didn't leave. When he hit Lucy, she finally ran. Ran until the country ran out. Until she came here, to this island at the edge.

The girl understands, of course. Harry hit her.

Alice has never mentioned family.

The girl lies between the white cotton sheets, feeling the flannel caressing her still-red, slightly itchy tattoo. Alone. The good thing about Harry was that he was always there in the morning, fetid breath and sweaty, but still, always there. Damn him. She wouldn't take him back if he begged. She sighs, reaching out of bed to pinch the needles of the knobby pine, rubbing the scent between her fingers.

The smell of trees is the smell of the man. The scent is enough to make her skin flush, to make her body respond.

Think of the way he looks at her:

Amazed. Gentle. Awestruck.

This is more than enough.

Days are empty and endless and eternal in winter. Cold white-grey light filtering through the windows like for ever. So much white. She shivers, gets up, stands naked under the hot shower, feeling the water pricking her back. Feels good. Like clean pain, not blurry like her ankle, like cramps.

She feels better, at once. A rush of good health. The Tylenol works hard.

She stands under the hot hot water, washing the clay down the drain. From a long way away she hears the knocking on her door of the other girls. Hurry up. We have to shower too. Hurry up.

The knocking is on her door. Knocking. She shakes her head vigorously. No past, only present, she reminds herself. Wraps herself carefully in a white towel robe, hair dripping, opens the door.

Wait, go back.

She heard knocking. Then what? She assumed it was the man, was ready for the man. Hot and wet, soapy. Walking towards the door (limping), robe hanging open.

On the doorstep, shivering — who?

The girl slams her robe shut.

On the doorstep, shivering — snow hard as rocks pelting down behind her like summer rain — is Alice. Crying. Tears squirting from her eyes. What?

Alice is saying something. There has been an accident.

This can't happen. Can it? The roads are so slippery, ice under snow. Cars leap and roll onto sidewalks. What is she saying? The girl squints at Alice as though this will make her hear better. She faints.

The funeral is next Friday, Alice was explaining. I know she would want you there.

Then nothing, just the wood floor, cold, with a puddle of water. Her cheek resting in the puddle of water.

Start again:

There was an accident in the car. Such a big car. It slipped, kept slipping. Into the lamppost. Lucy was sleeping. Sound asleep. They had been to see Santa.

But I already took her, the girl said. Angry. We already went.

I didn't know!

So she had to be pried out of the car with the jaws of life. Jaws of death. Anyway, she was in the hospital. So little, with all the beeping monitors and tubes. And she didn't make it.

Such a quick ending.

Didn't make it?

Christmas trees!

In winter, my heart is made of snow.

The girl hops back into the bathroom, vomits up the Tylenol, dry heaving until blood drips between her teeth. The snowflakes on the blue spruce are bobbing in the wind.

Alice is gone. I've taken some Valium, she has said, her eyes dead. So I sound calm. But inside, you know, inside there is something ripping and tearing. Screaming. Inside, I don't know what it is. Monsters.

Her face, haunted.

Lucy is dead.

The girl lies perfectly still on the floor, naked. Windows wide open, cold air swooping into the apartment, papers lifting and turning like flocks of birds. The branches of the trees rustle and murmur, snowflakes of paper, twisting. No. No no no no no. The girl hears these words, then realizes that it is her own voice. Wailing.

You're an angel.

I know.

The skin on the girl's fingers is blue. Lucy is also probably blue, she muses.

In the spring, it is a flower!

Boys and girls come out to play.

The girl drinks half a bottle of Scotch, for warmth. Vomits some more, something satisfying in the burn of stomach acid dripping from her nose. She is sick, sicker, sickest. Vomiting nothing.

This is not pretty. Death is not pretty.

God

is not pretty.

The man phones, his habit. Needs his fix. She picks up the receiver but does not talk.

Hello?

Are you there?

(A sniff. Can he hear tears through the telephone wires?)

I'm coming over. What's wrong? What is it? Are you OK?

She hangs up, replacing the receiver so gently, as though it were made of glass.

It will be OK. He's coming over. Sit and stare at white walls. Do nothing. Do something. What? Clean. Clean the bathroom, omitting gloves. The bleach burns her hand and smells like dying.

Barefoot in the snow, she walks down the steps to Alice's apartment. The door is slightly ajar. She goes into the living room and removes all the Disney tapes that the child had loved so much. She takes them. Also, the child's mittens. Why wasn't she wearing them? Her hands must have been cold. She takes the mittens and the movies back upstairs.

When the man arrives she is watching, singing, the words tumbling out, the words choking her. Her voice is flat and lifeless.

Lucy was only four years old, she explains. Four. She loved Disney. The man hugs her tightly to his chest, and together they watch *Aladdin. The Little Mermaid. 101 Dalmatians. The Lion King.*

Weep.

The girl cries so deeply, so many tears. She wonders if there are any left, is there a finite amount of saline? Soon, maybe all that there will be is blood, and red streaks will pour from her tear ducts. Soon.

The phone rings, and both man and girl only stare. The man is thinking about his grandchildren: this is wrong, he thinks, it goes against nature's order.

It should never be the children.

The girl eventually falls asleep, her grief too heavy for her waking thoughts. The man sleeps.

After a death, sleep is much deeper. As though in sleep, you can reach the dead person, if you sink into it far enough. It's as close as you can come.

It draws you down.

The wife is in the greenhouse, looking down the rows and rows of seedlings. So many trees! She has been in and out of three of these seemingly identical buildings, looking for her husband. The lights are out, but there is a weak winter sun, occasionally seeping through the snowy clouds. In each greenhouse, the seedlings are at different stages of development. As though in going from one to another, time has passed, the trees are taller.

She goes into his office, sees her paintings around the room on the floor. Why did I stop painting? she wonders. When did it happen?

In his small greenhouse, where he does his research, she pauses. The side of her husband that longs to create such beautiful things is foreign to her. Where is he?

Where are you, goddamnit? she asks the empty room. Through the glass wall, she can see a handful of men outside, working amongst the trees, shaking snow from the branches so that they do not collapse under the weight. She realizes that she does not know a single one of them, couldn't call them by name if she wanted to.

Where are you?

She goes back up to the warm cave of the house and reaches automatically for the phone. Listens to her daughter talk of morning sickness and saltines. Complain that her husband isn't as excited as she over the imminent birth. Speaks of Christmas and travelling on icy roads. She calls her Steven up north and chats to each grandchild in turn: even the littlest boy who can only coo and gurgle.

Are you all right, Ma?

Fine, just fine.

She calls Derek. Listens as he tells her of a silver-haired gentleman he would like to invite to Christmas dinner.

I mean, he says, we have only been out once, but it just feels right, you know?

Yes. Of course. I don't think Christmas, though, remember your father.

Which of course makes her think of her husband: where is he?

It gets dark so early in the afternoon, that it takes her a while to realize that it is nine o'clock at night. She has knitted three scarves — long yellow scarves with red trim at the end. Has she eaten supper? She doesn't remember.

Could she be getting that old? So old she cannot remember eating, or not eating?

Time heals all wounds.

Time and tide wait for no man.

Time keeps on slipping into the future.

It is eleven o'clock. Where is he?

The wife phones the police to see if there have been any accidents involving a 1995 red pickup. No. She calls the hospitals. No. She does not tell her children.

It would be admitting failure. Wouldn't it?

The man is drowning in his dream. He dreams himself younger, adolescent, swimming in the river behind his parents' farm. He dreams a current, cold and clear. There is someone he is trying to save. No. There is someone from whom he must escape.

Who is it?

His son. His face morphing and twisting. His grandson. His wife. She pushes down on his head. The water is angrier, foaming. He sees bubbles. He feels the cold.

The man wakes up with a start, sweating. The girl is so firmly entwined in his arms that he does not want to shift and wake her up. Tears have left red tracks on her cheeks. Every once in a while, instead of snoring, she gives a half-sob.

Dear God.

It shouldn't happen to the children.

The snowflakes twist and turn on the trees. The man drifts back into sleep again. He will hold onto the girl until he is strong again.

No. Until she is strong again.

The wife sits up all night, staring into the cold unlit fireplace. Damn him all to hell. Damn him. She imagines him dead: perhaps he has fallen down, heart attack, perhaps he is out in the trees somewhere. Perhaps she should go look.

No.

She knows that this is not true.

It is Saturday night, and it is almost midnight.

She plans the confrontation. What will she say? There is nothing left to say. A chill starts at the back of her neck, strangles her breath. He has left her with nothing to say. Why?

She has no choices left.

She packs his bags for him. Sits there alone for ever, for the rest of her life. Without him. The father of her children. Is he so important? Yes. She has given him the lead role in her life, without him, there is nothing.

She unpacks his bags.

The smell of clean laundry comforts her.

She leaves the suitcase out, just in case she changes her mind.

She plans an icy silence. She will not speak to him until he speaks to her, first. Childish? Maybe. He must know she is angry.

How could he do this?

Are you having another affair?

She packs her own bag. Sweaters, pants. Jewellery. The jewellery stops her cold. Pearls he gave her. Diamonds. Gold chains. What was he hoping to buy? Eternal love?

Of course, there is no such thing.

In the bottom of the box, a clay bracelet that Jamie made in kindergarten.

Weep.

Allow yourself to weep — something has been irrefutably lost.

She unpacks her bags.

Where would she go?

Up north, to Steven. East, to Jamie. Across town, to Derek.

She has nowhere to go.

Fuck, she says. She has never used that word before, it tastes bitter and solid on her lips. Fuck. Fuck. Fuck.

It is five o'clock in the morning.

Why does time seem to jerk by in hours, not minutes? Each time she looks at the clock, it is one hour later.

In the apartment on Faithful Street, the girl rolls over, only to find herself pinned in place by the man's arms. Her nose is stuffed up, and it is hard to breathe. His body is so hot against her skin. Like a fever. She slams a door inside against the pain, shutting Lucy out. Wiggles out from the man's embrace and stands by the open window, gulping in lungfuls of odourless cold air, a starving person swallowing food.

Lucy is dead.

The man sleeps between her white cotton sheets. He snores, tenderly.

Outside, the sun is rising. Traffic hums by, sporadically. Downstairs, a violin is being tuned. Everything goes on.

Does it?

Look at the man, sleeping. Mouth half open, arms hanging over the side. Does he belong here, trapped in her white sheets, in her white rooms?

Watch him sleeping.

Is this what she wants?

She lies next to him. Curls her body towards him. Half-asleep, he responds. Of course, he responds. His fingers trace the branches of the tree, burning into her spine. He strokes her skin. Rolls over on top of her. Crushing her. Tears stream down her cheeks.

Lucy:

in the winter my heart is made of snow! Christmas trees!

Still, he continues. He thinks he is healing her. Is he? She lets herself be comforted, suddenly aware: it is morning, and he is here. Sunday. Sunday is traditionally a terrible day to be the other woman. Sunday belongs to family. Family.

She floats back into dreamless sleep, waking to hear his voice murmuring in her ear:

Good-morning, sleepy one. Wake up. It is morning. Let me fix you coffee, breakfast. Let me shower with you, I will wash your back. Let me hold you.

Is he really saying this?

No, that is a dream.

He is saying:

Oh my God — what have we done? What am I going to tell my wife?

The girl rolls over as far as she can to the edge of the bed and feigns sleep while he stumbles around for clothes and keys. Stumbles around for a lie, an explanation.

There is an imprint of his head on the pillow. A dampness. His scent hangs in the room like a shadow.

She listens as the door closes behind him, listens to the surprising silence, emptiness, listens to the echo of the empty room. Wife. Always the wife.

Lunacy loops through her soul.

The wife.

It is not possible to cry any more, instead, she curls into a small ball amongst the nest of sheets and blankets. Makes herself so small as to be invisible. Feels her skin pull tightly down her painted back.

She closes her eyes, to make herself vanish.

The tree is his mark on her. It stings and burns. She is marked.

When the phone rings, she answers heavily, voice caked with sleep:

Yes.

Breathing fills her ear.

Harry?

Click. Dial-tone hums.

Harry. She closes her eyes. What does that mean? Her heart beats heavily, alive with new fears. Harry. Against her eyelids, she sees him standing above her, fist raised.

This memory has obliterated all the others.

Black-and-blue blossom seeping down her cheek.

That is not love.

There was no one before the man. Not even Harry.

Her hands reach around her body, tracing the very ends of the branches that twine around the soaring bones of her ribs.

Only him.

Miles away, Harry holds the phone in his hand and smiles. Did she answer? His fingers dialled the numbers. He waited minutes after dialling, then severed the connection. Did she know it was him?

Spread over the hotel bedspread, he admires the pictures of the gaping mouthed sharks. Whites. He was never alive until he was in that cage. He has to tell her. The girl will understand.

Blood and flesh cling to the teeth of the shark. No. That must be a trick of the light. The fish are beautiful. The water so blue against the white and grey.

Did she know it was him?

He imagines her lips moving: Harry?

The photos are glossy and overwhelming. Mouths, teeth, and eyes.

The wife is sleeping when the man comes home.

I got drunk, says the man, to her motionless expanse of flannel-covered back. I got drunk, before you ask, I got drunk and I stayed over at a hotel. I couldn't drive. I couldn't call — it was late and snowing. So save your breath.

He slams out of the room, pounding the door twice to get the desired effect.

Liar, the wife whispers.

Is it better to avoid the truth?

Or look too closely and destroy everything?

Like termites working away at the foundation of a house, how long can you pretend you don't see the sawdust, before the building sways and topples in on itself?

Liar.

The day flows by like a river, confined to its banks.

The man, as a penance, does not call the girl, works amongst his trees, feels thc silence around him, magnified by the fallen snow and ice-cold air; he works without real purpose, accomplishing nothing, eventually stopping and just walking. Walking, feeling muscles in his legs and back working, sensing the pull and push of ligaments and joints.

Alive.

Breathe in and out.

Smell the trees, and the snow and ice.

Smell the silence.

Sometimes the pain in his chest flares and dies, a match held up to the wind.

The wife stays inside the house, making lists. Christmas presents, groceries, things to do. Her eyes are red-veined, broken. She opens a box of Christmas cards and dutifully starts filling in envelopes, name, address, postal code lined up in little boxes to save postage. The curtains are open, and she stares up at the expanse of sky, and wonders if every winter is this cold, if the clouds are always this dark, if the days are always this short. If she has somehow forgotten to look up before.

The phone does not ring.

Where is he? Where is he? Where is he?

She won't go to him.

Walk.

The girl walks and walks, ankle pinching under heavy boots. Walks and walks, talking to no one. Acknowledging no one. At the ocean, the waves are, astonishingly, gone. The black sea stares back at her balefully, motionless. The snow on the beach is melted, the pebbles glisten grey and black. It is so dark. How did it get so dark?

She sees Derek ahead on the sidewalk but does not call out. He looks back. Does he? His eyes are on her, she feels it. What is he saying? Is he talking to her? He is far away in a crowd of people. She ignores him, walks on and on and on, until her lungs start to ache from the cold, and her tears freeze on her cheeks and her muscles burn from moving against the icy current of the air.

She carefully piles up her research material for the shark story. Lines up all the edges. Places it in the fireplace. Strikes the match.

What was she thinking? Sharks are Harry's territory. Not hers. She wouldn't want him to think ...

No.

She doesn't want to write any more.

When she closes her eyes she sees Lucy. In the mirror Lucy looks back at her. She is becoming the child. Is that possible? Pretend. Madness.

Am I crazy? Words whispered to herself. Mad as a hatter, says Lucy, laughing in the mirror. Crazy.

In winter my heart is made of snow.

Walk.

Her tired feet follow Derek to the museum. Deserted. It's winter, after all.

Her face feels pinched and pulled, as though it has been moulded out of clay and not allowed to dry properly, moisture seeping in and creating cracks. Lucy loved the museum. The animal displays, the woolly mammoth forever poised one foot ready to take a step. (Is it real? they heard a tourist ask once, how do you feed it?) The magnificent skeleton of whale bones, suspended from the ceiling as though swimming, fleshless, through water so light it has become air. The smells of the old town: gasoline and dust and applesauce. Captain Cook's boat, with its tiny bunks and lamps still lit. The Indian displays: the long house, the masks that frighten her, the beating of the drums.

Harry always said he wasn't that kind of Indian.

No? What kind of Indian are you?

The kind that was raised by white men.

Look:

Lucy loved the water wheel, the old barn, the coal mine. What an amazing place, the museum. The girl sits in the fake train station and watches the fake trains roar by.

Derek and his new lover pull open the heavy museum doors. Jeremy. That is the other man's name. Jeremy.

Yes?

Oh, nothing.

Jeremy is a historian. He works in the museum. He wants to show Derek everything. The floors and floors of storage. Behind the exhibits. Derek's heart skips a beat when he examines the back of Jeremy's neck. Perfect silver hairs, cut to perfection. Perfect.

Is this love?

How lonely do you have to be before you snap?

It's almost Christmas.

The girl dials defiantly from the pay phone in the lobby.

How did it go, she says, with the wife?

Silence.

Are you there?

Yes. It was fine. She ...

Yes?

She doesn't know, suspect, I don't think.

Oh.

I don't know ... I don't think ... Maybe we shouldn't see each other for a while.

Pardon? I can't hear you.

I said —

Listen, I'm at the museum. Come and meet me? Please?

Hang up, quickly. Minimize the damage.

I'll meet you.

The world is so tiny, minuscule. People running around on a tiny rubber ball inevitably will run into each other. Bodies, careering around their days, sooner or later must collide. Is that a rule of physics? A tiny round sphere covered with plants and water and weather.

Always weather.

Will spring ever come?

Bang.

On his way to the museum, the man gets a flat tire. No spare. He walks to a gas station, repairs cost him a hundred dollars. Despite the sun it is cold and the walk has tired him out. Perhaps this is why he lets his guard down, allows himself to be happy that it is bright and blue although it is winter, it is bright, and he is going to meet the girl, the magnificent beautiful girl, her looks only slightly marred by the strange tattoo that clamours over her back like a swarm of black insects.

His girl. His beautiful girl.

Feel young. Brush off fatigue with a shrug.

Maybe we shouldn't see each other for a while.

The world is so small, spinning on its axis. Perhaps it is the spinning that pushes people together at the most unlikely times.

Behind the exhibit, Derek looks out, hidden behind the backdrop.

Hey, he says, seeing the girl. I know her.

Oh?

Well, not really.

Jeremy pulls him close. His heart sighs. Sinks into his lips.

Ah.

The girl waits on a bench.

Wait:

Something is wrong.

Her body is bent forward. Hands pressing abdomen.

What is it?

The man rushes to meet her.

I'm late, sorry ... I ... What's wrong?

Cramps, she says through gritted teeth. That's all.

When she stands, her body folds.

Cramps?

Behind the exhibit, Derek and Jeremy step apart, breathing heavily.

Well, says Jeremy.

I know, says Derek.

But wait. Something catches his eye? Is that ... could it be?

Dad?

What?

Derek pushes Jeremy away. Hang on, he whispers. Eyes fixed forward.

How can the man not feel the eyes of his boy (can we go camping, Dad, can we? can we get a dog, a cat? Dad? can I borrow the car, Dad?) — how can he not sense something in the air? Accusation. Shock. Disbelief. Anger.

How can he not notice?

The man helps the girl into the empty lobby, past the waterfall curtain and the model of the longboat filled with explorers from a different time.

Yes, we'll have to get you home into a hot bath, he says gravely. The situation is urgent.

Derek blinks, turns back to Jeremy.

Sorry, he says. Thought I saw someone else that I knew.

The truck cab smells like soil and exhaust. The seat is slippery. The girl slides closer to the man, so she has something to hold on to. She pretends she doesn't notice when he pulls away.

Look out the window:

The winter sun is weak. Is that a shadow? Lucy, waving. Lucy, running.

Look again:

Nothing. Suburban yards, tipped white with ice. Slushy brown snow, melting.

I keep seeing Lucy, she says. I see her everywhere.

I know, it's OK. That's normal. (Is it?)

It's not normal that she died. So young.

I know.

She was my best friend, the girl says quietly. So quietly the man does not hear her over the whoosh and roar of the passing traffic.

It's Thursday. The wife is kneeling in the hospital chapel.

She sits apart from the family and friends. She can hear her own voice, whispering prayers. Her knees creak against the hard tile floor.

The man takes the girl to his own house, daring fate to bring his wife home early. What else can happen?

Fills his own tub with steaming water. Unfreezes his wife's chicken soup to heat on the stove. Feels his blood run cold. What is he doing? He wants the girl so badly. Will this lust ever fade to nothing? Feelings muddy his thoughts. Lust. Love. He had been so resolute.

Maybe we shouldn't see each other for a while.

His children's faces mock him from the refrigerator door. From the mantel. From the wall. His hand trembles.

Think about this:

The earth spins so fast that one minute you are a boy then a man then a husband. Try to remember the transitions. The choices. The love.

Maybe there was none. Until now. The girl in the steaming tub, hair damp and clinging to her cheeks. Her back black and painted, details wrought in black ink. Her gift to him.

Remember the gifts.

Love. His fear softens and warms his icy flesh. Love.

Maybe he has earned this, maybe this is what he deserves.

He can almost believe that, crossing into the foggy bathroom. He can almost believe that as he lowers his body in the water with hers.

She does not tell him how much it hurts.

Downstairs a door slams, and the girl jumps. Groping for clothes. Footsteps move around the lower floor.

Dad?

Just taking a bath. Steven?

His erection vanishes in a heartbeat. His hands pull away from her skin.

Silence.

The screen door screeches, then bangs.

Here is another memory:

The girl is four or five. She lies in bed, sweating, trapped under the weight of Winnie the Pooh bedclothes, so heavy that they are suffocating. Downstairs, the sound of voices: her mother and father? No, her father and someone else. A man.

Did this really happen?

The voices are angry, accusing. You promised. No I didn't. Yes, you did. Well, I can't leave now — I have a child. So? Leave her. No. Yes. Leave that woman and that child: you belong with me. No. Yes. Maybe ... Damnit, get out! No. I will never leave you.

The child lies in bed, listening, twisting out from under Eeyore and Roo. Struggling. Why are they yelling? Daddy! Mommy! Daddy! MOMMY!

Running footsteps, her father, dishevelled, a shadow behind him. The other man? Who is he? The child crying, her father rocking and rocking until the tears stop. His tears. The child's dry up much more quickly, and she watches in amazement this man's face melting into a pool of watery pain.

He's gone, her father says, simply. Now he's gone.

Where is Mommy? Mommy!

But he doesn't answer, just rocks and stares.

Mommy!

He leaves the room, leaves her alone still knotted into the bedclothes, and it is several hours, or maybe minutes, before she hears the front door open and close and her mother's voice calling — anyone home? Where is everyone?

Where did that come from?

The girl dresses, hurriedly, in the man's bedroom. Opens the closet. Has to look. A row of men's shirts, ironed. Dresses and coloured silk blouses. Of course. She breathes the scent of lavender and old shoe leather. Dry cleaning and plastic bags. Breathes in the wool of hand-knit sweaters, unworn suits.

The man's voice mingles with his son's. Out the window, she watches them embrace, clapping each other on the back. The voices drift up to her, suffocating.

Lay low for a while, he told her. Wait in the truck. I'll take you home.

No.

She has crossed some boundary, unseen. But it's not her fault. He brought her here. Didn't he?

She goes out the side door. To wait. Steps out onto the icy ground. Her breath dances in clouds, trees swirl and tilt in the wind. She wanders up and down the rows, the naked summer and spring trees all look the same in winter, yet the evergreens rise above, sweatered in green wool knit of needles. She walks down a small valley, a creek, frozen solid, snakes by under her feet. Walks farther, until the house is just a light behind her. The property is peppered with mature growth, trees with trunks a dozen feet around, reaching up, protecting the smaller. She is dizzy from walking and from cold and probably hunger, but she keeps going.

Why?

Why not? Because it is winter and cold and angry and calm and empty and echoing with the scent of new growth and fallen snow. Because.

Now is the winter of our discontent.

Watch a bird fly by, hopping from tree to tree, looking for shelter, or food.

Wait in the truck.

She is not welcome here.

She tries to close the truck door so quietly. Doesn't she? The bang reverberates through the air.

The man winces.

In the cab of the truck, the air is thick and fetid. Breathe. Why does she feel so dizzy? Look up, into the sun. A bird flies by. A bird? A fairy? She reaches up towards the flying doll, reaches up. Blinded by the sun. An angel?

As a very young child, she remembers making angel wings, attaching them to the backs of her dolls, suspending them from the ceiling. Those aren't angels, her sister told her, scathingly. They're dolls. Angels aren't real.

No?

What did the girl see just before she fell asleep? A smattering of light, only a drop in blood pressure, a gossamer pattern on the back of her closed eyes.

The truck must be gone before the little blue car pulls in. The man makes excuses to his son.

No problem, Dad.

He drives her home. The silence feels angry. The girl doesn't speak.

All the same, they climb the stairs together. All the same, once inside, clothes come off. Naked. The sight of her young white body, bones protruding hungrily from her hips, dark nipples rising like chestnuts from perfectly small, freckled breasts. The sight of that stirs him so much that he has to take her, has to hold her one more time. Has to finish what was started, before.

Just for a minute, he says, holding her tightly, pushing into her. Just for a minute, he moans.

I don't know ... I don't think ... Maybe we shouldn't see each other for a while.

Chapter 9

Christmas is a joyous season. Isn't it?
It's for the children.

At Lucy's funeral, it rains. So cold that the rain falls frozen, immutable, like diamonds crashing onto the roof of the church. So many people. Did the child know these people? No. Of course not, friends of the parents, the grandparents.

An assortment of people.

It is easy to pick out Alice's friends. Too much makeup, too much hair.

Tears mingle with the guests.

The girl rocks back and forth on the wooden pew, feeling the cold wood through her thin black skirt. The skirt is covered with a pattern of tiny leaves. These, she traces with the end of her narrow white finger. Humming under her breath.

Look around at all the people, dabbing their eyes as the priest — whom the child never could have met — reads comfort and prayer from the open bible.

... I walk through the valley of the shadow of death I feel no evil for

thou art with me ...

Later in the proceedings, Alice sings. (Not her usual performance, thinks the girl, cruelly, in spite of herself.) Her voice rises, thin and reedy in the resonant church, interrupted by the hammering of ice pellets on the ceiling. If rain is God crying, then what is this, this hail of frozen tears? God has turned to ice. She breathes more deeply, feels Alice's singing vibrate through the building.

She hates funerals.

Who doesn't?

Suicide

is a sin.

There is a hushed ceremony at the graveside. The girl watches her sister, to see how she should act. Her sister weeps softly. Her grandfather collapses in the grass and weeps inconsolably, great hiccuping sobs wrack the ground he lies on. The girl wants to lie down, too. Her legs stay frozen in place. It is raining, but it is summer. Water runs warm down her face. She does not need to cry her own tears.

Her mother is lowered into a deep, rectangular hole. Ashes to ashes, intoned the priest, dust to dust.

Suicide is a sin.

The girl goes back to school the next day. Aware that she is different now from all her friends. They isolate her with sympathy.

Wait:

There is more to this story.

There were two bodies in the car. Daddy?

A catch — he isn't dead. Not quite. Not technically. They are able to save him. The girl thinks, oh, now he is free. Wonders if he will go to the man, the voice from downstairs. Wonders. Now what?

It isn't like that, of course. He should have died. Institutionalized, his eyes are always wide open. It's the first time the girl is able to examine his face without a camera obscuring her view. His eyes are dead. His heart pumps: oxygen in, carbon dioxide out. Keeps filtering away the toxins, keeps processing the energy.

She doesn't visit:

suicide is a sin.

In winter, my heart is made of snow, Lucy says.

Oh?

In spring, it grows a flower!

Spring will never come.

The girl leaves the black-haired Barbie under the wooden pew.

She wants to run and dance and scream and sing and fuck and love and burn and sleep. All these things! To be alive!

The girl has been holding her breath all winter. Leaving the church, a flood of oxygen pours into her lungs. To run! Her ankle, only slightly stiff in her high-heeled shoes. Imagines running up and down the rows of trees. She is wearing a long black skirt, flecked with leaves. Running up and down the rows. Running in high black shoes, the suede ruined by the jagged cold ground.

Amazing grace, how sweet the sound, that saved a wretch like me ...

Angels drift on scarves of silk.

She can't run yet. It's too soon.

Harry's plane shudders and drops. How many miles? Drops down through the air, soundlessly. People probably scream. He looks around, smiling. The frightened drop their heads between their knees. Harry looks out the window towards the blue water, wishing for a tank, a regulator. A mask.

He imagines the plane cutting through the waves, sinking down. The compartment filling with water, fresh, salty, cold.

He imagines gills forming on his cheeks, fins rising from belly and spine. Teeth growing angrily. Inner eyelids. Harry closes his eyes. His jaw loosens.

The plane levels out, dangerously low. Is it dangerous?

The fasten seatbelt sign blinks off. Flight attendants pass around pillows and blankets, collect bags filled with air sickness and fear.

Harry sighs. Not this time.

What is he yearning for?

The man has left the girl a message.

Listen:

He has to go away. His daughter is in the hospital. Cramping. She might lose the baby. They want to be with her. She may need them to help out. Does she understand?

He'll call her when he gets back.

Merry Christmas, if he doesn't see her.

Merry Christmas?

Her own belly has ceased cramping. The blood never came. It is as though the whole tide of menstruation began, then pulled back. She does not examine the reasons. Cramping. The ice-sun streams in through the hazy white curtains and illuminates the dust on the floor. Has winter always gone on this long?

Winter began early this year.

She is light, weightless, as she packs her bags. She barely exists, just a wisp of a girl with a black ink drawing filling the white canvas of her back. She has been left with no other choice.

What would you do?

The man holds his wife's hand outside his daughter's room.

The doctor emerges.

Well?

She'll be fine. Bed rest. She can go home.

False alarm.

He squeezes his wife's hand. A sigh travels through his heart. A pain he hasn't been aware of disappears.

The wife looks longingly down the hall towards the chapel. Prayers beckon. Singing. Close your eyes and open up your heart to God. Now is not the time — he wouldn't understand.

How does the girl know where they are going?

His house, always open. Calendars, diaries, address books.

It's awkward for her to get in. Steven and his family are there, filling up all the rooms. A hundred kids. Three kids, young enough to be everywhere at once. She has to wait a long time at the bottom of the driveway in the twins' car.

It is too easy to find. Printed on a card taped above the phone. Too simple.

Is this wrong, what she is doing? She thinks that it is love.

Isn't it?

It is the only warmth in this bottomless season. His fingers are spring. His love is the sun. Like a plant, she must seek warmth. She must.

It is about survival.

He won't like to be away from the trees, she thinks. They are so vulnerable in winter. The wife should have gone without him. Should have let him stay. She did it on purpose. To take him away from the girl.

Cover his eyes:

Don't look, I'll tell you when it is over. So wifely, so protective.

The girl copies down the information from the card. Flips open the calendar. Calendars always tell the truths: reservation numbers, flights.

Is it obsession?

Do you believe in angels?

The man is, of course, all she has left.

She packs her bags, takes the ferry instead of flying. Cheaper, and more satisfying. The grey-white waves churn out behind the bathtub boat. Sharks swim invisibly under the hull. This comforts the girl. The sharks. Not the crowds of green and red of holiday travellers, so much green and red. Don't people wear black any more? Her fingers pull on the collar of her white shirt.

The man and his wife flew, to be there more quickly. Think of the flight to California, the man's hand on her leg. Will he rest his hand on his wife's fleshy thigh?

Perhaps he has been lying to her.

Jealousy is a monster, a spiky tailed iguana, it has just been born from the egg she has carefully been hatching, flicking its poison tail and disappearing into the crowd.

(Could we get a blanket, please?

His hand resting on her crotch, his wife of thirty years.)

A shaking is creeping over her, a tiny tremble in her cells.

Celebrate:

It's the man's birthday.

The man is leaning over his cake in Jamie's dining room, laughing at the amount of candles, dripping wax onto the dark chocolate glaze. Through the lens of the camera his wife holds, he looks the same as he did as a teenage boy, denim shirt and jeans, hair brushed just so, eyes sparkling in the flame.

There is no difference, really, just a pattern of lines tracing all that they have been through.

Around Jamie's table: Dylan, his hand reaching out to place a silly hat on his father-in-law's head; the man, raising a glass of wine to his lips; the wife, camera poised, the words from happy birthday just fading from her lips; Jamie, obediently staying reclined on a La-Z-Boy imported from the living room.

Laughter chokes out all the oxygen.

Try to breathe.

This is family.

Family. This is all there is, isn't it? The man is here, fully in this room, with these people. Then an image of the girl leaps in front of him, onto the table in front of him, and the sparkle fades from his eyes, and something closer to a grimace pulls at the corner of his lips.

A feeling that might be regret. Or remorse.

Does he miss her?

The walls close in. His wife is taking up too much room. He is trapped. Her voice is an off-key soprano lilt: happy birthday to you, happy birthday to you, happy birthday to my husband, happy birthday to you.

He excuses himself abruptly.

In the bathroom, he splashes lukewarm water on his face. Again. Water trickles down behind the collar of his shirt. Down the hall, a phone. A lifeline. Fingers pulse the familiar numbers.

I don't know ... I don't think ... Maybe we shouldn't see each other for a while.

He wants to take it back. Is it too late? The words are already out there, already voiced. They have been given importance.

They are growing bigger and gaining strength.

Who are you calling, Dad?

Hang up, quickly. Bite back the obvious retort — I'm not your Dad. No.

No one. Steven, actually. Just checking in.

Smile.

The man claps his son-in-law on the back. Quite a party, he says, considering. I'm so glad about Jamie. I couldn't have a better gift.

This, he means.

Most of the time, he is lying.

After dinner, the wife feeds all the leftovers in the fridge to the dog, heaping pork roast, roast beef, chicken stew into his bowl. Everything she could find in the fridge.

You love me, now, don't you, she whispers into his ragged fur.

The man watches with disgust.

The girl twirls around the room, unseen, the tree on her back gently moving as if blown in a storm. Muscles climb like vines up its solid trunk, around her ribs and spine.

Opening his gifts, the man tries to smile and nod where appropriate. Shirts and ties. Books.

What does his expression give away?

Sorry, Dad, Jamie says quietly. I didn't mean to spoil your birthday.

What? No. No, you didn't. This is ... great.

He lets the girl slip away, as if in a dream.

His son-in-law gives him golf clubs.

I don't play, he says, surprised.

I thought you might want to try something new, Dylan answers, affronted.

I would, thinks the man, *a new life.*

Great, he says. Great idea.

His wife gives him a camera.

Another new hobby? He enquires, jaw working.

I just thought ...

Never mind, it's great. Really. I've been meaning to get one. Now I can take lots of pictures of my next grand-baby.

He smiles and reaches over, rubbing his daughter's protruding belly. Hot, like molten fever. Shocked at how warm and soft it is, so unlike the concave, white, coolness of the girl. Shocking.

His wife's face begins to fold on itself: after all these years, his words can strike a blow. Tears.

El Niño has brought another blizzard. Outside, white swirls down and around and down, obliterating vision.

The man and his wife had planned to go to Hawaii for their honeymoon, but at the wedding, blood began to drip on the floor under the full white skirt of the wife's wedding dress. Blood, slithering down her white stockings, dripping steadily in a rust-coloured river onto her white satin shoes. Blood that would have been their oldest son, or daughter. And the honeymoon had been cancelled.

Jamie lies in the bed. The flow of her blood has been stopped. The baby clings firmly inside. She did not inherit her mother's bad luck.

It does not run in the family.

The wind howls across the water. Waves pound on the island shore. The trees bend, and snap.

The electricity flickers. Darkness descends. And then another flicker. Light.

Derek is writing a new symphony. The staff lays blank in front of him. The tiny black notes are still in his head. He hums, softly. In the kitchen, Jeremy is making tea. Milk and sugar? he calls.

No. Nothing.

Domestic bliss. Derek's pencil hovers above the waiting lines, trembling. From the time the music plays inside his head, until the time the notes appear on the paper, he is terrified. Afraid that if he sneezes, or speaks, or God forbid, laughs, it will all disappear. Bang. His hand trembles. Marks appear on the paper. With one hand, he plays the notes on the piano. More notes. More. The symphony begins to take shape. His tea grows cold.

Hours later, hours, he is still frozen in place. Jeremy touches his neck gently.

Massage?

No. He slaps the hand away.

The music in his head begins to fade.

See what you've done? You can't interrupt!

Why is he so angry? Slam out of the house, bang as many doors as possible.

Drive away.

Derek stops at a bar and has a drink. Two. It's his father's birthday. If he calls, he knows his Dad will hang up on him.

Happy birthday, Dad, he lifts his glass. The bar that he is in would curl his father's hair.

Men dressed as women. Women as men. Men and men and more men, embracing to a silent drum beat.

An awful truth:

Jeremy looks like his father.

Sick, isn't it? A twisted grin plasters itself horribly across his face. Jeremy.

My dearest love sprung from my only hate.

Drink more. It's the answer to everything. It's an answer. His father by the fire, downing one Scotch after another. The son learned well.

He has enough drinks to gain the courage required to pick up a young boy on a corner, and drive into an alley. An exchange: love for money. Or is it just release?

Drive.

The roads are plagued with ice black as coal. Camouflaged by midnight. The power pole looms up from nowhere. Four city blocks are knocked into darkness. Derek falls asleep. Slips into a nightmare so deep it is undisturbed by the flashing red lights and mournful wail of the ambulance.

When he finally comes around, in the crowded emergency room, they ask him who to call. No one, he says. No one.

Sleep it off, cowboy, says the nurse, slipping the curtains closed around him.

No one.

He imagines his mother, always so worried, rushing to his bedside. His father, scornful and angry.

Falls asleep to the sound of a stomach being pumped in the next curtained cubicle. It should hurt, the doctor is saying. Serves you right for swallowing to begin with.

He can't sleep here, among the damned.

His licence has been revoked. He gets out of bed and hails a cab. So easy, to walk away. When he gets home, Jeremy is gone.

He can tell immediately. From the streets, he sees the emptiness reverberating around the house like a halo.

Of course.

Happy Birthday, Dad.

Harry's plane touches down at the airport. The passengers applaud. There is barely a jolt as the rubber hits the frozen ground.

At first, it is surprising, to be this cold after such a long time away. But by the second breath, it all comes back.

Home.

He takes a bus into town, watches the familiar houses float by through the steamy windows. The bus is full, but he does not look at anyone. It is all silence to him, silence and breath-fogged glass. He transfers downtown, his pack taking up an entire seat. A hundred pounds of dirty laundry and camera supplies. This bus will take him directly to the university, to his office, to his files.

His office is just as he left it, locked. The air is stale. There is food in the garbage which has rotted, the stench assails his nostrils. His pen is lying on his notebook exactly where it was when he left.

The small shark in the salt water tank is dead. He forgot to get someone to come in and feed him.

Starved.

Belly up.

A shark will die if it stops swimming. It needs to move to keep oxygen flowing past the gills and into the bloodstream.

If it stops, it's all over.

Carefully he puts his shark pictures into his filing drawer. Then, as an afterthought, he fishes out the smelly corpse and puts it in there too. Let them figure that one out, he thinks.

Harry is feeling a little crazy.

Maybe it's the weather, this merciless cold. His fingers are still tingling from the change from cold outside to warm inside. They are red and burning. His feet itch.

El Niño is changing everything.

The girl — who has slept in a hotel she cannot afford in a room heavy with the smell of smoke and exhaust and other people's laundry — awakens to the roar of traffic and wind streaming in the window and does not remember where she is. The curtains buck and shiver.

The bedspread is green and worn almost gold in places, the carpet also green, but slightly mottled, as though so many stains have left it marked for life, for ever. Green. Green seeps into her pores and becomes nausea.

She is exhausted.

She cannot sleep.

The air in the room is strange and damp. Her hair frizzes around her face, in a wild halo. This colour green is inhuman. Her eyes shudder.

She yearns for a drink or a library. A place to hide.

A cup of coffee.

Remember why she has come:

Being in the same city as the man dulls the roar that has filled her silences. She packs up and checks out. Her hair is wild around her head, like Medusa. Medusa's ugly stepsister.

Her cheeks are hollow.

She has read somewhere that after a period of time, pain messages sent down the same chain of nerves eventually will shut off. The message has been given, and ignored.

So?

The cramps are gone. Are they?

Or just forgotten.

She cannot rent a car in this weather. No one is on the road.

The cab drives by Jamie's house, slipping and sliding. For one horrifying moment, it glides towards the ditch. The girl imagines trying to explain her presence. Crazy.

The house is ordinarily small and suburban. A dog barks in the yard.

The cab takes her back to the hotel. She checks in like she has never been there before. The man behind the desk pretends not to recognize her.

Do you have any rooms that aren't green? she asks.

For her trouble, she gets a room painted orange, with wallpaper showing underneath the paint.

She dreams:

She is in the school chapel, staring up at the glory of stained glass panels stretching forever above her head, the colours of sunlight blocked by glass. She kneels in the confessional, fabric worn from so many students' knees, and spills out her sins, her sins filling the tiny room. Sins. The room gets smaller. They do not feel like sins as they drop from her parted lips, one after another. They feel like love. They flap around the booth, strange misshapen butterflies.

She wants to sing in this church, taste her own voice resonating off all the magnificent walls.

Instead, kneeling again before the statue of the virgin Mary, she rattles off her penance. Catholic school detention. Four Our Fathers, eight Hail Marys, two cups of flour and stir until done.

Waking, sitting, something — a fluttering in her head — a tracing of lights that are not coming in the window. Do you believe in fairies? No. Only the strange fireworks that come from kneeling, then standing too quickly in dreams.

The blizzard stops. El Niño rests.

The overflowing bus carries the girl back to the ferry, nested between the fetid breath of one passenger, the body odour of another.

On the ferry, she escapes outside. The air is hauntingly still. The water glassy and black, placid. The blast of the ferry horn almost knocks her to her knees.

The cigarette trembles between her lips.

She watches the islands slide by, blanketed by the dark green of uncut forests, the houses with smoke wafting from the chimneys.

It is all so beautiful, and desolate.

That will kill you, says a voice to her left.

So there he is, all of him, smelling faintly of the alcohol that is still escaping from his pores, and a little of sweat and soap and coffee. Smelling so familiar, and whole.

Relief. Sweet relief! To be discovered, to find each other.

Happy Birthday, the girl says.

It's not my birthday.

It was.

Yes.

Why are you here?

I wanted to surprise you.

You did. I am surprised. I am ...

What?

Surprised.

The man and girl fold so neatly into each other's arms, you would think that they were one person, accidentally separated by some tremor in the universe. Touching and whispering, her hair becoming smooth under his touch. His headache receding into nothing. Nothing.

Through her coat, his fingers burn into the black tracing of branches on her back: branded, he whispers.

What?

Nothing.

They are not hidden from the view of the passengers inside.

What are they thinking?

Remembering:

Where are you going?

I'm with my wife.

Oh.

It's not a choice.

So go.

You're angry.

No.

Yes, you are.

Just tired, go.

Go quickly, before the tears spill over the girl's cheeks. Bless me father for I have sinned.

Once, he took the three children to Hawaii for two weeks, while his wife was recovering from an appendectomy. She didn't want them to worry, so obligingly, he packed them up. Took them away through the sky to this place that they could not have imagined. Spent his days teaching them to swim in the high surf, his tiny children, clinging to his hands. Each night they would cluster around the phone to tell their mother of the day's adventure. Daddy took us to the beach. Daddy danced the hula. Daddy built a castle out of sand. Daddy.

How far can Daddy go, protected by this love? This adoration?

Would they forgive him?

No, of course not.

What price is too high?

What would a girl so young want with a man like him, getting so much older every day?

Walking away, he thinks: she followed me.

Should he be afraid?

What he feels is closer to pride.

Or anger.

Or love.

The girl leans over the guardrail and watches the water thrusting out behind the boat in a white-foam wake. She is calm. Serene. Loved.

At night, he tries to make love to his wife, and fails. Hangover, he mumbles. Old age.

His wife tries not to be disappointed. Waits until he is sleeping and stands in front of the full length mirror and inspects the pouchy whiteness of her stomach, the purple and blue weavings of her veins. Recoils from her own touch.

Back home, Jamie is bent over double on the couch. Cramps, she says between gritted teeth, that's all.

Her husband holds her hand, letting her squeeze until he is sure he hears his bones breaking, a sound heard from the inside.

We should go to the hospital, sweetie.

No, Dylan! It's just a cramp.

Blood drips out. Like mother, like daughter?

Rest, says the doctor. You haven't lost the baby. Bed rest. I mean it this time.

Before, was he joking?

Remembering the blood that stained the shiny white shoes, dripped onto the church floor at the wedding thirty years ago, they don't phone her parents.

Jamie lies in her bed and thinks of the bleeding: how could she not? There is a baby, curled inside her uterus, the size of what? She doesn't know. A lima bean. A tea bag. What? Fighting to get out? Or stay in. She breathes deeply, hoping to translate the rush of oxygen to the fetus, breathe baby, breathe. She lies still. Legs clamped together. Close all exits.

Outside the window, it is dark. Which means that it could be any time, any time at all in this dark winter.

Now is the winter of our discontent.

Now. Is the winter of our discontent.

Let go.

Drift into an uneasy sleep. Dream of sand, a tiny baby with huge eyes sinking into the sand. Her hands, desperately sifting, trying to find the fetal child. Big eyes filled with sand and tears. Hot sand running through her fingers, again and again.

From the bottom drawer of the filing cabinet, Harry retrieves the gun and points it towards his head.

No.

That doesn't happen.

Harry retrieves the gun and cradling it carefully at first, he strokes it like a kitten. It smells cold and oily. Places it in the pocket of his pack, making the pack impossibly heavy. The gun doesn't weigh that much.

The cold metal has burnt his finger tips. What is it he is forgetting?

Chapter 10

Christmas Eve.

The girl is where she always is — in the mirror, looking back. Has she always looked this awful? Spidery black branches creep over her back. White skin on white bone on white on white. Black circles pool fatigue under limpid eyes.

Strange how she hasn't noticed before.

Does the man notice?

Wind rustles the white snowflakes, cut by a child's hand.

Remember the following:

When the girl first met the man, she was fresh and clean. Now, bearing his mark, she is bent and sad. He is angry. She is spent. Love may be a firecracker, fizzling spectacular patterns against black-velvet night skies.

Then what? A used shell, smouldering on the ground.

She wouldn't change a minute. He would relive them all. Can they both sense the shifting of the seismic plates? Something is about to change.

They still have not run out of things to say.

Love may be a fire-log, artificially lit by chemicals to burn strong and full until fading into ash.

The phone brings them together:

What are you doing?

Lighting a fire. Thinking of you.

And later?

Waiting for you. What are you doing?

Waiting for them to leave. Waiting for them to arrive. Waiting to see you again.

They talk about the future as if there is one.

There is not even a Spring.

Look:

They walk hand in hand down the sidewalk, crowded with Christmas shoppers rushing, panicking. One last toy. One more thing. They are oblivious. She looks up at him and he does not see her shadowy sleep circles. He sees himself.

Watch how they touch each other's sleeves, arms. How they stop to kiss, gently, amidst the seething crowd.

Go with them into the diner:

Steam pours upwards from bowls of thick soup chunky with meat and vegetables and salt. They look at each other across the arborite table. Change positions, sliding together onto a vinyl bench.

Laughing and talking. About what?

All their conversations are flirtations.

At her apartment, he makes love to her angrily, banging her up against the wall. She is lifted from the ground. He spins her round and round. His sex is angry, hot, and red. She bites back her cries. Furniture bangs.

He makes love to her gently.

Downstairs the violins stop.

For the first time, he isn't able to finish. Fakes it. Pretends to bellow and collapse on her tiny breaking bird bones. Artifice pollutes the room. Of course, she knows, but says nothing. What would she say?

At the door a small box pressed into her hand:

Promises sparkle in a stone that could cut glass.

Merry Christmas.

Wait!

He's already gone. The stairs bear the brunt of his footsteps.

Merry Christmas.

The ring weighs down her finger, slips and slides provocatively. Christmas Eve.

The clock hovers in the afternoon. Time unchanging.

Everything changing.

In a mall at Christmas, you are never alone. The girl finds herself wandering, dizzily, amongst the listless shoppers. She didn't buy the man a gift. The stone throbs on her finger, keeps sliding around, towards her palm. She clenches her fist and feels it biting her flesh.

Sweaters and books are too impersonal. She has nothing left to give.

The roads are dangerously slippery — the crowds thin, heading home before it becomes too unsafe. She wanders through the echoing mall.

I'd like a haircut.

We're just about to close.

Please, I need ... for Christmas.

It's all right, a boy says quietly. I'll do it.

The scissors against her neck release her. Her head lifts and floats above the season. Anything else?

The shop is deserted. He is in no hurry to leave.

I don't know.

What would you like to try? In your wildest imagination?

They share some bourbon and forget everything.

Bleach lifts the brown out of her hair like an eraser wiping clean a mistake. More and more. Rinses through her hair the white of silver. Her short curly hair glows under the fluorescent lights.

The haircut makes her smaller.

Thank you.

No, thank you.

She walks to the mall doors, floating. Has to be let out by the security guard. Doors are locked. Everyone has gone home.

She calls her sister in IdahoIowaOhio. No answer. Family. What's the point?

Downstairs, the violins churn out tired Christmas carols. Don't they ever stop?

The ring twinkles spitefully in the candlelight. Wearing the ring of a married man. She twists it round and round. Shakes her hand and feels it bounce against her knuckle. Harry didn't give her a ring. Gave her a bracelet instead. Silver. Heavy. Heavy like Harry. Carved Indian bracelet.

Harry would do anything to deny his past, after all, he was a white Indian. That's what he said. Raised by white foster parents in an all-white suburb. What did Harry know about being an Indian? She threw the bracelet after him when he left. It bounced against the cement, rattling. Of course, he couldn't hear it.

He wouldn't hear it.

She didn't stop to look where it landed.

Harry rents a car. Why not? Drives around the city on roads made of accidents and ice and slush and debris. Christmas lights flash unrepentantly. He drives to his foster parents' house and sits in the driveway. Watching.

The pipe/gun/bottle in his father's hand comes down on his mother's head like a benediction. Harry hides in the corner, watching. His mother screams. Again and again. What can he do? Harry is just a little boy. His father whoops and hollers.

Harry can't stand to hear it, so he turns the volume off. Harry is two years old. Why turn it back on? Silence is thick and warm like a blanket.

Harry was saved by suburbia.

From what?

His real family.

Harry's foster father is a marine biologist. Took Harry on his first dive. The first invitation into the silent blue-green kingdom where hands moved in silent languages and silver-bright fish flicked by under the glass surface. It was so much, it was too much.

It wasn't enough:

When Harry was a teenager, he was so angry. So full of rage.

I hate you, he said — bellowed — to his white parents.

They were so surprised, they let him walk away.

The car idles in the driveway, the exhaust shimmering thickly in the cold.

Inside, he can almost hear the warmth — the fireplace crackling, the tree hung with antique baubles handed down through the generations, the loneliness.

A family scene:

The man's family clusters into the living room, children hanging off the arms of sofas and chairs. The air is laced with eggnog and fireplace smoke and of course pine needles. The giant tree reaches up towards the ceiling. The wife serves drinks and hors d'oeuvres, perfect pastry snails clutching spiced meat hearts. Jamie smiles indulgently at the children, the bulge in her own belly resting lightly under her hand.

Is this enough? The diamonds in the room sparkle possessively. His wife. His daughter. His daughter-in-law.

Did he really give the girl a diamond? Boxed promise he cannot keep.

She'll never forgive him. He tastes her salt on his lips. Shudders. Voices rise and fall like ocean waves, gaining momentum. He can't hear them.

What? What did you say?

Leave the room. Go outside where it is possible to breathe. The trees exhale oxygen into the ice-still night. O holy night the stars are brightly shining ...

What's wrong with Dad?

Yeah, Mom. What's wrong with Dad?

I don't know.

I do.

Steven, please. Don't spoil Christmas.

Mom ...

Mom ...

How did this come to be her fault?

Ice cubes tinkle in glasses.

The girl goes downstairs and lets herself into the twins' apartment. The room is full of people she has never seen before. All in white shirts and black pants. Piles of instruments take up most of the space in the living room.

Standing between the twins, she realizes they could be her siblings. Small, lithe, blond curly hair shining silver in the lamplight. They smile and laugh, embrace her, wish her a Merry Christmas. Bring her a drink. It is all so normal.

So normal.

A pink flush fills her cheeks.

Everyone in the room is so young.

She curls herself into a chair in the corner to watch.

The twins had a party when Harry left. They told her it was for her, to make her feel better. It tasted more like a wake.

It is close to Hallowe'en, so for some reason the twins see no reason not to make it a theme party.

Harry is gone.

(His fist hovered over her like winter. Eye blossomed black like a storm cloud.)

The house is full of people in ghoulish black costumes, eating bags of Hallowe'en candy in between taking drags of joints and swilling back the punch, which is sickly sweet and sticky and is mostly pooled on the floor.

The girl feels sick. She wants the room to be full of quiet people, respectful, like those at a funeral. It is a funeral, but they don't know.

Perhaps this is when she started to hate them.

Funeral for a baby that didn't get born. His fist over her. How could she? The fetus popped out into the doctor's vacuum as though it wanted to go. As though it was relieved.

What did she do? Hates Harry now. The baby gone, she is empty and unforgiven. What could she have done?

Alone and broken. She can't be blamed.

She didn't tell Harry about the baby because he would have looked away and pretended he didn't see her lips moving. Or worse — laughed his thick, heavy boiling-water laugh. Disbelief or cruelty.

The girl pushes her way out of the crowded party living room, and finds that the party has moved into her apartment, too. Door unlocked, it's all one big house. Lucy is dressed up as a bumblebee. Asleep on a pile of coats. She goes into her room and two people she doesn't know are having sex in her bed.

They are naked, except for the masks.

She is glad Harry is gone.

The party is a tidal wave that has crashed over the house, and all the marine life, out of water, is much louder than you would have expected. Starfish screaming, a cacophony of cod.

The girl hated diving because everything was always moving. Every time you looked over your shoulder something new was there. He used to want to swim way out deep, hoping to see sharks.

That was before El Niño, before the sharks swam silently, deeply, north through the warming water.

Why aren't you in a costume? Boozy breath floats towards the girl's nose.

Fuck off, she says.

The girl drinks until the baby floats away.

She sits on the stairs, at the top, so she has somewhere to fall if she tips over.

One of the twins passes her on the stairs. She has never seen one without the other. Can I ask you something?

Sure.

What was so great about Harry?

You don't know?

No.

But you married him.

Yes.

He was so ... strong. We knew him before. In high school. He used to

... protect us. From bullies. You know?

Oh.

Anyway, he says, we'll get your mind off it. We've got something planned.

Sure. Great.

The stairs tilt drunkenly below her.

She thinks she tries to say something but sees only bubbles rising from her mouth. Presses her forehead against the cold stucco wall.

What was in the punch?

The twin goes by again.

We're going to have a hunt, he announces. Candy hunt. In the basement.

I know, she says, not unkindly. The other one already told me.

Can't they see she is in mourning?

There is someone sitting next to her on the stairs. She can't see him because her hair has fallen forward. Can't lift her arm to move it back. Strong smell of sweet cologne.

Come here often, he says, after about ten minutes of nothing. Or maybe it was longer.

Live here, she says.

I see. Quite a party.

Huh. Hair falls thick and fast between them. She can't see anything. Seaweed waving in the current.

I have to admit, he says, I wasn't invited.

Great. Neither was anyone else.

Why?

Funeral.

This?

Yes. It's a funeral.

I see.

Sit in Polo-drenched silence, the walls undulating around them, stairs writhing like electric eels.

The girl's tongue is a piece of bull kelp in her mouth, sweeping listlessly from side to side in the shallows. She is crying, face wet and salty.

His fist so far above her, falling and falling and

falling.

He should have been a ballerina. There was something in the way that he moved, muscles and sinews lining up to lift each limb.

Before he left, the twins were teaching him to play the piano. He couldn't. Notes came out monotone and lifeless, like his voice.

What was in the punch? She floats underwater forever, where it is silent and smooth and forgiving. Imagines the fetus swimming away, impatiently — angel fish.

One of the twins shouts: things are hidden downstairs! Come and find your prize!

There is the general pounding of feet in the direction of downstairs. A couple rushes by the girl hand in hand, and she is crushed by loneliness.

Who are these people?

People dressed in black are pouring out the front door like octopus ink. They are carrying things. She can see clearly. They are carrying the TV. A chair. A suitcase. Someone is carrying her flippers under his arm. Her scuba tank. Harry's black suit. Great prizes, they exclaim. Great!

The twins did not specify that what was hidden was candy.

She wants to tell them to stop, but her mouth will not open. Can't open her mouth this deep down — her regulator would slip free of her lips and she would be left opening and closing like a fish, trying impossibly to suck the oxygen from the water.

The girl closes her eyes and lets the party swirl on around her. The diamond on her finger feels like a warning. Storm approaching.

Checks outside — it's too dark to tell.

She loved the way the man's voice cracked, nervously, when he spoke to her. It was everything.

In the living room of the man's house, liquor is flowing freely. The children have been put to bed

visions of sugarplums dancing in their heads.

The wife tucks them in.

In the living room, liquor is heating up the room. Voices are rising, higher and higher. Not in song.

It's Christmas, please don't do this now — Jamie pleading.

No, let's. Dad, anything to say?

Am I on trial? In my own house?

Maybe you are.

Dad?

Dad?

Are you having another affair?

The man leaves the room. Tries to storm out of the room but stumbles over the side table. What now? He goes into the bedroom and starts packing his suitcase.

Really?

Yes.

Packs his suitcase, while his wife puts the children to bed. She reads them "The Night Before Christmas".

One more time, please? Please?

All right, but this is the last time.

Steps outside, suitcase in hand.

Jamie's voice: Don't do this, Dad, please not on Christmas.

Steven: Let him go.

Derek: What about Mom?

How could she not hear what is going on one floor below, through paper-thin floors?

He carries his suitcase out into the night, slipping on the glacial driveway. Gets as far as the greenhouse before he realizes that he's not going to leave. He can't leave. There was never a possibility. The roots of family grow too deep, too strong, stronger than sex, stronger than everything. Stronger than love.

Goes into his office, leaves the lights off. Under the starlight, looks out the windows over the rows and rows and rows of trees, roots bound into the ice-cold earth, holding

on

for dear life.

Where's your father?

Oh, Mom.

What? What is it?

Mom ...

What have you done?

Silent Night Holy Night all is calm all is bright ...

I'll get him, Derek says quietly. I know where he's gone.

Does he?

Derek drives slowly into the city towards Faithful Street. The roads are deserted.

Look up into the starry night:

He half expects to see Santa flying by with eight tiny reindeer. This isn't for you, Dad, he says to the empty seat beside him. It's for Mom.

How does he know where she lives?

Trees delivered in silver buckets. For a friend.

Following her down streets and paths from the rocky shore. It's easy, so easy, to follow without being seen. She of all people should know this. She brought his father to the museum to show him. Look, Derek, watch.

Cold pierces his skin through the closed windows.

City sidewalks busy sidewalks dressed in holiday cheer ...

Harry slows the car in the alley behind the house on Faithful Street. Lights are blazing inside. He smiles. A party.

His fingers stroke the metal gun.

Don't look in the mirror, you'll see what you've become.

The man stares out the office window into his valley of roots and feels himself being pulled down into the floor his feet and legs

working their way
firmly down into the
earth.

His research mocks him from the table. Everything that has

been forgotten since he met the girl.

It was a mistake.

It can't be undone.

It's clear to him now. It's just too late. The now-familiar pain sears through his chest.

Derek climbs the stairs towards the apartment, pausing at the window of the party. Musicians playing their instruments with wild abandon. For a minute he stops, the chords of his own symphony beat a finale in his blood. He has to write it down. The ending has just come to him now. Paper.

He climbs the stairs at a run. The door is open.

Go in.

Why not?

He grabs paper and without fear lets the music pour out, the pencil steady in his hand.

Harry watches as the man enters the apartment without knocking. Releases the safety. Now he knows why he came. Does he want her back?

What does he really want?

Bump. The shark drives into the steel cage. The cage vibrates. The predator eyes its prey. The tumblers slip into place.

The girl is so tired. Her eyes droop shut amid the music and merriment. A hand on her shoulder. Wake up. Are you all right?

Yes ... just tired.

She goes back up to her own apartment, her white haven perched atop the disintegrating structure on Faithful Street.

Screams — then:

Oh. What are you doing here?

Derek is drunk on liquor and the music. Holds it up: Look! It's finished. I've finally finished.

But what ...

Oh. That. Well, I came for my father?

Your father?

Yes. My father: Oliver.

Oliver. (The diamond ring tightens on her finger.)

My father. You knew he was.

Yes. I knew. I'm sorry.

It doesn't matter. Where is he?

He's not here. He ... I ...

It's not for me. It's for my mother. I can't let this happen.

It's all right ... Let me ask you this. Have you ever been in love?

Me? I ...

I love your father.

An impasse. Of course.

If you love someone, set them free.

A hand, not seeming to be her own, reaches out and presses the ring into his palm. Tell him.

What?

Tell him it was my idea. (Her voice breaks. Broken.) Tell him not to call.

Do you mean it?

No. But you'd better go, before I change ...

(Bang. The shark smashes into the vibrating steel, jaws open, second eyelids rolled down to protect his eyes from the adrenalin-pumped attack of the struggling prey.)

Bang.

The door swings open:

Harry? Harry ...

Catches sight of himself in the mirror down the hall, gun raised, the safety is already off. Wild black hair swirling around his head, brown face squinting. His father is in the mirror, gun raised. His father.

Bang.

Of course, Harry could not hear the bullet leaving, but he could certainly feel the kick of the steel, the ceasing of vibration as the music stops.

Everything stops.

The girl and Derek watch.

Watch:

As the mirror shatters to the ground and Harry looks at no one and stumbles slipping of course because it is so icy down the stairs down and down and down and probably should have broken his neck but somehow doesn't and manages to get to the car before his hands start shaking and shaking and shaking.

The wife finds her husband in his office, surveying his kingdom, his back to her.

Just tell me, she asks. Are you going to leave?

He doesn't answer. Can't answer. But can shake his head slowly back and forth, shake his head, no.

Maybe we shouldn't see each other for a while.

I don't know if I will be able to forgive you. Not this time.

Nods his head. Yes, he knows.

The crescent moon hangs in a sliver up in the sky, hanging from invisible threads. The blade of a scythe. The middle C.

We'll talk it out. After Christmas. Christmas is for the children.

Nodding, nodding
while the pain spreads into his jaw.

That's all then, says Derek, clutching his papers and the ring and stepping over the shards of glass. Has to shout because their ears are still ringing. That's all.

Yes, she answers. I guess it is.

In the distance, there is a blue-red wail of sirens. She catches sight of herself in a broken piece of glass on the floor. Silver-white hair, white white skin. Luminous eyes.

Bends over to pick it up and feels the first soft flutter in her womb.

Epilogue

Did I tell you my name? I don't think I did. It had no meaning until your husband spoke it:

Nina.

It was never much of a name before. And now — when I am moving along the sidewalk, summer sun searing over my newly shorn scalp forming my sweat — it carries me along. Ni-na. Ni-na. Ni-na.

It never meant anything before.

I want you to know that I loved him and I gave him back and I want you to think of that when you look at him.

When he comes to you at night.

When you feel the heat of him pressing into you while you are sleeping.

I want you to think:

she gave him back.

How is he? Oliver. I want to know but if I get close enough to ask I might not let him go again. He gave me a ring, you know. I gave it back.

That was a lot.

I thought the movement in my womb was a second chance. Now I wear the gossamer silk of angel wings over my bald scalp so people don't stare with pity. I've learned to find hope in small things: music, running, the blue blue sky. Derek helps. Has he told you of our friendship? No.

Never tell.

He wouldn't.

Do you know how close you came to losing him to a stranger's bullet? AIDS is nothing held up against one angry piece of molten lead, splintering.

I hate you, because I am going to die, and you have all I ever wanted.

Spring did come, but not in the way I had hoped.

I don't see Harry. I hear he's fine. It was a "psychotic break", the doctors said. Interesting, don't you think? I saw him on PBS, talking about the white sharks off the coast of Vancouver Island.

I never saw Alice again.

I think Derek is in love with the twins. I don't know which one, but I could never tell them apart. He seems so happy, so boyish. It's contagious. I feel better every day, even as my body betrays me.

Being alone tastes sweet like aspartame — not satisfying, but comforting all the same.

I think of your little blue car ricocheting off the road and I look forward to winter again. Derek tells me all this hate will make me sicker.

To you, it was just another affair. That is not what it was to Oliver. It can't have been all it was.

Hope springs eternal.

Hope is merely disappointment deferred.

Waiting and hoping are the whole of life, and as soon as a dream is realized it is destroyed.

Someone said that. I think it was an Italian: Minotti. In Italian, it was probably even more beautiful, like music.

I never went back to the tattoo parlour, to get the leaves added to the tree. The shadow of a leafless winter rides on my back wherever I go. The roots have sunk into my muscles, my tissues. It has become a part of me.

The cold dark season.

The hopeful tree.

El Niño is giving us a hot hot summer to make up for the bitter long winter. The seagulls refuse to fly. They stand in the small shade, motionless, like statues. The grass is all dead and yellow and smells like burning.

People stay inside breathing the chemical ice air of machines and cursing El Niño.

I run along the cliffs and my feet bite into the dust, sending it up in clouds, choking me. The cliffs are steep and sharp, a simple step to the left and I would go over. I remember:

it's not the fear of falling, it's the fear of jumping.

I keep running. Down the stairs, the endless stairs that lead down and down and down still farther. Feet find the beach and pebbles slip and slide out of my way. The sky is so blue and blue and blue and so the sea is blue. The sea is only a reflection of the sky. My legs are machines, pistons, rhythmic. The ground turns to sand, the sand pulls my feet sideways, the muscles in my legs stretch to accommodate. The sea shines everywhere into my eyes like diamonds. Today it is calm, and I breathe deeply to saturate my lungs with this serenity and into my blood flows more hope, piggybacking on red blood cells laced with poison medicine.

Sometimes, I go to the convalescent home and sit with my father. He is not there, he is already gone. I study his features, and look for something. For nothing.

The machines beep.

I have his lips.

I stop and throw up behind a log, though there is no one else there to see.

I miss Oliver so much. Did I tell you that? It is an agony that riddles me with pain. I wake up at night, sobbing. Does he miss me too?

No. I don't want to know that, either.

I like to think the choice was mine to make.

When my hair fell out, it was still silver-blonde.

The scar across my belly is a scythe, middle C, the thumbnail of a moon.

The sky has been blue for months.
Winter will never come.